THE CONFESSION

Look for more
heart-stopping stories from

FEAR STREET....

The Perfect Date

Secret Admirer

Runaway

Night Games

FEAR STREET

THE CONFESSION

R.L. STINE

SIMON PULSE

New York London Toronto Sydney New Delhi

SIMON PULSE

An imprint of Simon & Schuster Children's Publishing Division

1230 Avenue of the Americas, New York, New York 10020

This Simon Pulse paperback edition July 2022

Text copyright © 1996 by Parachute Press, Inc.

Cover illustration copyright © 2022 by Marie Bergeron

FEAR STREET is a registered trademark of Parachute Press, Inc.

All rights reserved, including the right of reproduction in whole or in part in any form.

SIMON PULSE and colophon are registered trademarks of Simon & Schuster, Inc.

For information about special discounts for bulk purchases, please contact Simon & Schuster Special Sales at 1-866-506-1949 or business@simonandschuster.com.

The Simon & Schuster Speakers Bureau can bring authors to your live event.

For more information or to book an event contact the Simon & Schuster Speakers Bureau at 1-866-248-3049 or visit our website at www.simonspeakers.com.

Series designed by Sarah Creech

Cover designed by Heather Palisi

Interior designed by Tom Daly

The text of this book was set in Excelsior LT Std.

Printed and bound by CPI Group (UK) Ltd, Croydon CR0 4YY

10 9 8 7 6 5 4 3 2 1

Library of Congress Control Number 2022931940

ISBN 9781665921039 (pbk)

ISBN 9781442466432 (ebook)

1

What would you do if one of your best friends took you aside and said he had a confession to make?

What if your friend confessed to you that he *killed* someone? And he begged you not to tell anyone. He begged you to keep his horrible secret.

What would you do?

Tell his parents? Call the police? Try to convince him to tell his parents? Tell *your* parents?

Or keep the secret?

Not an easy choice—*is* it? I'm seventeen and sometimes I think I know a lot of answers. But when a really close friend called our group to his house and confessed to a murder in front of all of us—well . . . what could we do?

I'll tell you one thing: On that warm spring day last May when my friends Hillary Walker and

Taylor Snook came to my house after school, we did not have murder on our minds.

The air smelled so fresh and sweet. Bright green leaves were uncurling on the old trees in my backyard. And rows of red and yellow tulips swayed gently in the flower bed beside the garage.

The whole backyard shimmered under the bright afternoon sunlight. Hillary, Taylor, and I dropped our backpacks on the grass and sat on them, stretching out our legs, raising our faces to the sun.

Taylor tugged her wavy, white-blond hair back from her face. Her green eyes sparkled in the sunlight. She shut them and tilted her face to the sun. "Julie, have you ever sunbathed nude?" she asked me.

The question made Hillary and me laugh. Taylor was always trying to shock us.

"You mean in the backyard?" I asked.

"No. On a beach," Taylor replied sharply. She had no patience for my dumb questions. Taylor was a new friend. Sometimes I had the feeling she didn't really like me that much.

"One winter, my parents took me to an island in the Caribbean called St. Croix, and we went to a nude beach there," Taylor said, eyes still shut, smiling at the memory.

"And did you take off your swimsuit?" Hillary asked.

Taylor snickered. "I was only seven."

All three of us laughed.

Hillary climbed to her feet, her dark brown skin glistening with sweat. The long, single braid she always wears swayed behind her head.

"Julie, could we go inside?" she asked me. "I'm melting out here!"

I raised my hand so that Hillary could help pull me up. "Can't you ever stay in one place for more than five minutes?" I scolded her.

Hillary and I have been friends since junior high. So I'm used to her. But I think other people are surprised by how tense she is. How fast she talks. How her eyes are always darting back and forth behind those white plastic-rimmed glasses she wears.

She is intense. That's the only word for Hillary. She is smart and nice and funny and . . . *intense*.

She reminds me of one of those wind-up toys that's been wound up too tightly and goes off—too fast—in all directions at once.

Anyway, she tugged me to my feet. And the three of us dragged our backpacks into the house. We settled around the round, yellow kitchen table, with cans of Mountain Dew and a bowl of tortilla chips.

And naturally we started talking about boys. Vincent and Sandy, mostly.

Vincent Freedman is another one of our group. Another really old friend of mine. I have to confess that recently I've wished he were more than a friend. I really think Vincent and I could be a great couple. Or something.

But that's another story.

I don't think Vincent has the tiniest idea that I have a major thing about him. Not a clue.

Sandy Miller, another good friend, has been going out with Taylor for about a month. That's how Taylor got to be part of our group.

Poor Sandy. He's been dazed and confused ever since Taylor got interested in him. No lie.

He's so shy and quiet, and not exactly considered a major babe at Shadyside High. I think he's in shock that a girl so beautiful—so *hot*—seems to be into him.

Lucky guy, huh? Well, to tell you the truth, Hillary and I are just as surprised by Taylor's choice as Sandy is.

But that's another story too.

So we sat around the kitchen table, talking about boys and laughing a lot. And then we started talking about the party. *The* party.

A party at Reva Dalby's house is a big deal.

Reva is the richest girl at Shadyside High. Her father owns at least a hundred department stores. And they live in an enormous stone mansion in North Hills with guard dogs and tall hedges all around.

Reva invited the whole senior class. And she's hired *two* bands to play in the backyard—a garage band called Garage Band that plays at the local dance club, Red Heat, all the time. And a hip-hop group called 2Ruff4U that's flying all the way in from L.A. just for the party—at least that's what Reva tells everyone.

Reva isn't the nicest person we know. I mean, no one would vote her Miss Congeniality at our school. But who cares? We're all dying—*dying*—to go to her party!

So we were talking about the party. And Hillary was fretting about what to wear. "The party is outside, right?" she was saying. "And it still gets pretty cool at night. But I don't want to wear anything too heavy. I mean, I plan to dance a lot. So if I wear long sleeves or a sweater . . ."

I tuned out at that point. It was typical Hillary, worrying herself into a frenzy, talking so fast, it was impossible to get a word in.

She was still talking when we heard a bumping noise at the kitchen door.

I jumped up as someone pulled the storm door open without knocking. A tall figure barged into the kitchen.

All three of us cried out.

And that's when all the trouble began.

2

"Hey, Al—don't knock or anything," I said angrily, rolling my eyes.

Al Freed snickered. He lumbered up to the table, grinning his lopsided grin at us. "What's happening, girls?"

"You're *not* happening!" Hillary snapped instantly. "You're *definitely* not happening."

Taylor and I laughed, but Al didn't think it was funny.

Al is also a senior at Shadyside High. He is big and blond and kind of tough-looking.

With his tiny, round blue eyes set close together around a big beak of a nose, he always reminds me of a vulture about to pounce on his prey.

He always wears black, like a vulture. And his lip is always curled in a sneer, as if he's trying to show the whole world just how tough he is.

I know I make him seem kind of creepy. But actually, Al used to be part of our group. We all liked him a lot. But then he started hanging out with some "hard dudes" from Waynesbridge. Really bad-news characters.

Al changed. He started drinking a lot of beer. At least, that's what I heard from some other guys who know him. And he started getting into trouble. I mean, serious police-type trouble.

Too bad. Whenever I see Al, I remember the way he used to be, and I wish he could forget his new friends and go back to the way he was.

But I don't think that ever happens—do you?

Al stepped up to the kitchen table. "I can tell that you girls were talking about me," he teased. He narrowed his tiny eyes at Taylor. "You're hot for me, aren't you?"

"You've got *that* wrong," Taylor replied coldly. Her green eyes can go as cold as marble when she wants them to.

"You know you want to dump Sandy and come riding with me," Al insisted, practically drooling on her.

"What kind of a tricycle are you riding these days?" Hillary cracked.

I told you. Hillary is real quick.

Al's big ears turned red. That's how you can tell when he's angry.

I didn't see that he had a can of beer in his hand until he tilted it to his mouth. He took a long swallow, lowered the can, and burped.

"You sure know how to impress a girl," Taylor cracked.

Hillary tapped her long purple fingernails nervously on the tabletop. The sunlight from the window reflected off her glasses, but I could see she was watching Al carefully.

I think she's a little afraid of Al now. I know I am.

He slid the beer can into the crook of his arm, bent his arm, and crushed the can easily. "I've been working out," he told us.

"Bet you can crack walnuts between your teeth," Hillary muttered.

Al ignored her. He tossed the can across the room. It clattered into the sink, leaving a trail of beer droplets across the white linoleum.

"Hey—watch it!" I cried. "What do you want, Al? Why are you here?"

He turned his blue eyes on me. "You're my favorite, Julie. You're the best." He waved at Hillary and Taylor. "They're trash. But you're the best."

I rolled my eyes. "What do you *want*, Al?" I repeated impatiently.

"Twenty dollars," he said, sticking out his big

paw. It had black grease stains on it. His fingernails were caked with black dirt. He'd probably been fiddling with his car. "That's all. Just twenty bucks."

"I don't have it," I replied curtly. I crossed my arms over my chest. "Really."

"You're the best, Julie," Al insisted. He didn't lower his hand. He kept it in my face. "You're great. You're *awesome*. Twenty bucks. I wouldn't ask you unless I really needed it."

I uttered a cry of disgust. "Al, I'm totally broke," I told him. "And you already owe me twenty bucks."

"Go away, Al," Hillary chimed in. "Why don't you get a job?"

"Who would hire him?" Taylor asked sarcastically.

I was a little surprised that Taylor was joining in. She moved to Shadyside at Christmastime. She'd only been part of our group for a month. So she didn't really know Al well enough to be making cracks about him.

I guessed she just wanted to help me out.

Al pulled a vape pen from the pocket of his black flannel shirt.

"Hey—no way!" I shouted. I shoved him toward the door. "You know my parents don't allow vaping in this house!"

He danced away from me, grinning. He took a long drag and blew the vapor in my face.

"Give her a break, Al," Hillary insisted, climbing to her feet and pushing her chair out of the way. She and I both closed in on him.

"Hey, whoa!" He raised both hands as if trying to shield himself.

"Get out!" I cried. "If my mom comes home and smells that thing—"

He sneered as he narrowed his eyes at me. "Julie, your parents don't allow you to vape. But I know a little secret, don't I? You do it anyway."

"Shut up!" I insisted.

His sneer spread into a grin. "I saw you at the mall last weekend. Puff, puff, puff." He blew more vapor in my face. "Julie is bad. Julie is *baaaaad!* Maybe I should tell your mom. . . ."

"No way!" I shrieked.

Mom caught Hillary and me vaping in my room when we were in ninth grade, and she went ballistic. She promised me a reward—a thousand dollars—if I never did it again in her house.

I hate to think what my parents would do if they found out that sometimes I vape when I'm out with my friends. I know Mom would have a cow. It would get ugly. Real ugly.

And I knew Al wasn't kidding. He'd tell my

mom. Unless I stayed on his good side.

Which was why I loaned him the *first* twenty dollars.

"Al, I'm broke. I really am," I insisted.

"Yeah. Right," he answered.

"What do you need twenty dollars for, anyway?" Hillary demanded.

"So I can take Taylor out," he replied, grinning again.

"Ha-ha. Remind me to laugh," Taylor muttered. She stuck her tongue out at Al.

"I love it when you do that!" he told her.

She groaned and shook her head. "Grow up."

Al turned back to me. I didn't like the cold expression on his face. I never used to see that kind of hardness in him.

He pulled a tiny knife out of his pocket and flipped it open. "How about if I make some modifications to the table, Julie? Do you think you could find the twenty bucks then?"

"Al, please—" I started.

But he turned the knife between his fingers and started to lower it to the tabletop.

"Al—*don't*!" I screamed. I dove for him. But he swung around and blocked me from the table with his broad back.

He held the knife tip close to the yellow Formica.

"Come on, Julie. You can find twenty bucks. You don't want your mom to find a big scratch, do you?"

"Stop it! *Stop!*"

Hillary and I both pulled him away from the table. Al flipped the knife closed and started to laugh, an annoying, high-pitched giggle.

We pulled him toward the kitchen door. "Goodbye, Al," I said.

But he yanked himself free and turned to Hillary. "Your daddy is a big-deal doctor. I'll bet *you* have twenty dollars."

Hillary let go of him and sighed wearily. "Why would I give you anything?"

Al brought his face close to Hillary's ear. So close he could've bitten her dangling, orange glass earring. "Because of chemistry," Al whispered, loud enough for Taylor and me to hear.

Hillary gasped.

"You wouldn't want Mr. Marcuso to know you cheated on the chemistry final," Al told Hillary.

"You can't blackmail me!" Hillary insisted through clenched teeth.

Al laughed. "Of course I can! If I can't blackmail you, who can?"

"But you *gave* me last year's final exam!" Hillary protested. "I didn't ask you for it, Al. You *gave* it to me!"

"And you *used* it, didn't you?" Al asked, almost gleefully. "If some little birdie should tell Marcuso you cheated, Hillary, he'd flunk you. And then you wouldn't get into that fancy college that accepted you. Boo-hoo."

"Al, you used to be a nice guy," I said, shaking my head. "How did you get so obnoxious?"

He pulled my hair. "I studied you!" he shot back, laughing at his own cleverness.

"You really can't go around threatening people," Taylor chimed in. She hadn't budged from the table. I thought maybe she was using the table as a shield against Al.

"Yeah. Get out of here!" I insisted, shoving him again. "Really. Take a walk."

But Hillary was already digging into her bag. She pulled out a twenty-dollar bill and pushed it into Al's outstretched hand.

"When are you going to pay it back?" she asked. She didn't look at him. She kept her eyes down on her bag.

"Good question," Al replied, smirking. "Beats me." He jammed the money into the pocket of his black denim jeans. Then he turned to the door. "Have a nice day, girls!"

He took three steps—then stopped as my mom pulled open the glass storm door. "Oh—hi, Mrs.

Carlson." He couldn't hide his surprise. I saw his ears turn red again.

My mom stepped into the kitchen, carrying a brown grocery bag under each arm. "Hi, everyone. I'm home early."

Al took one of the bags and carried it to the counter for her.

Mom set the other bag down. She pushed back her hair. She has dark brown hair, like I do. And the same big, brown eyes. Our best feature.

"We don't see you around here much anymore," Mom said to Al.

"I've been kind of busy," Al replied. His ears were still bright red. He said goodbye and hurried out the door.

Mom turned to us. "Why is he dressed all in black?" she said. "Did somebody die?"

She didn't give any of us a chance to answer. Suddenly she narrowed her eyes and sniffed.

I instantly knew what she was about to say.

"Mom—" I started.

She put her hands on her hips, her face tightening in anger. "You've been vaping."

"It was Al!" I cried. "We weren't. It was Al!"

"That's the truth, Mrs. Carlson," Hillary said. She and Taylor both stood awkwardly at the table. I knew they wanted to fade away, to disappear.

They'd both seen my mother when she went into one of her flying rages.

"I don't care who it was, Julie," Mom said, clenching her jaw and speaking each word slowly and distinctly. "You're in charge while I'm away and—"

She moved over to the counter to unpack the groceries and gasped when she saw what was in the sink.

"A beer can, too?" she screeched.

"That's Al's!" Taylor and I cried in unison. I glimpsed Hillary shrinking back against the wall, trying to blend in with the flowery wallpaper.

"You just threw it into the sink?" Mom demanded shrilly.

I started to reply, but what was the point? I mean, I knew I was in major trouble.

It didn't matter that Al was the one doing these things. Ever since she caught Hillary and me in my bedroom three years ago, I don't think Mom has trusted me completely.

I'm sure she suspects that all kinds of things go on here while she's at work. And now, she came home and what did she find?

"Julie, I'm grounding you for the weekend," Mom said in a low voice. I could see her jaw muscles twitch. She talked softly because she was trying to control her anger.

"No! You can't do that!" I screeched. I didn't mean to sound so desperate, but how could I help it?

"The party!" I cried. "Reva's party! Mom—if you ground me, I'll miss the party!"

Mom raised a finger to her lips. "Not another word."

"You can't *do* this!" I wailed. "I'm seventeen years old and I won't—"

"I won't have your friends drinking beer and vaping while I'm not here," Mom shouted, losing control. "I don't care if the party is at Buckingham Palace! You're grounded. You're missing it. One more word, and I'll ground you for two *weeks*!"

I shook my fists in the air and let out a cry of rage. I could see Hillary and Taylor behind the table, both avoiding my eyes, both feeling embarrassed—and terribly sorry for me.

This is all Al's fault, I told myself. *He has become such a total creep. This is all his fault.*

What a horrible afternoon.

I think all three of us—Hillary, Taylor, and me—felt the same way. I think all three of us wanted to kill Al that afternoon.

Of course we had no way of knowing that Al would be dead in two weeks.

3

So I missed the party.

Will I ever forgive my mother? Maybe sometime in the next decade.

Hillary reported that it was the best party in the history of Shadyside High. She has a mean streak, that girl.

She could have told me that it was the most boring night of her life. Instead, she told me how awesome the two bands were. How she danced until two in the morning. And then had a late moonlight swim in the Dalbys' heated pool. How she never laughed so much in her life. And how everyone kept asking her where I was.

I told Hillary never to mention the party again. That was a week ago, and she kept her promise— until the two of us were walking to Sandy's house on Canyon Road after school on Friday.

We walked under low clouds, threatening rain. The air felt cold and wet, more like winter than spring.

"I just don't get it about Taylor and Sandy," Hillary started.

I shifted my backpack on my shoulders. It was loaded with homework for the weekend. "What about Taylor and Sandy?" I asked, thinking about my history term paper.

"Well, you should have seen them at Reva's party," Hillary continued.

I stopped walking and grabbed the sleeve of her blue sweater. "You promised. No talking about the party."

She tugged her arm free. "I'm not talking about the party, Julie. I'm talking about Taylor and Sandy."

"Well . . . what about them?" I asked grudgingly.

"I watched them at the party," Hillary replied. "It was pitiful. Sandy followed Taylor around like a lovesick puppy dog. And Taylor hardly talked to him. I mean, she was busy coming on to every other guy there."

"She likes to flirt," I agreed, jogging to cross the street before the light changed.

"It was disgusting," Hillary insisted. "You

should have seen the way she danced with Bobby Newkirk. And I saw her making out behind the garage with some boy I'd never seen before."

"Oh wow," I murmured. "And what did Sandy do?"

"Ran around getting her Cokes," Hillary reported. "I mean, I don't get it. He *had* to know what Taylor was doing. She was so obvious! She practically pretended Sandy wasn't there. And he just grinned at her and followed her around."

"That's true love," I said dryly.

"It's not funny," Hillary scolded me. "You know how serious Sandy can be."

"I wish Vincent could get serious," I muttered under my breath.

Hillary turned and squinted at me. "What did you say?"

"Oh, nothing." I sighed. I pictured Taylor flirting with guys at the party. I had tried flirting with Vincent. But he thought I was kidding or something. He just made jokes.

"Sandy is a great guy," Hillary continued. "But I think — "

"I actually think they're a great couple," I interrupted. "I mean, maybe Taylor can get Sandy to lighten up. He's so shy and quiet all the time. He's never really had a girlfriend before. He's so excited about it, maybe it will change him. Maybe . . ."

I waved to a station wagon full of kids from school. When they rumbled out of view, I caught the fretful expression on Hillary's face.

"I don't think Taylor is good for Sandy," she argued. "I think Sandy is going to get hurt. I think Taylor may dump him the first chance she gets."

"I know he's a lot more serious than she is," I agreed. "But aren't you being a little hard on Taylor?"

Hillary's mouth dropped open. "Excuse me? Hard on Taylor? What are you talking about?"

A strong wind greeted us as we turned onto Canyon Road. Sandy's redbrick house came into view on the next corner.

I had a feeling that Hillary might be a little jealous of Taylor. Before Taylor started going with Sandy, Hillary was the only other girl in our group. And now Taylor had arrived, with her trendy clothes, her perfect hair and perfect face—and perfect body. And Taylor quickly seemed to focus all of the group's attention on her.

So maybe Hillary was just the tiniest bit jealous.

But as I walked beside her on the sidewalk to Sandy's house, I decided not to mention this theory of mine. It would only hurt her feelings. And she'd spend the rest of the week denying it.

"Taylor is okay," I said instead. "She's not a bad girl. She likes to have fun, that's all. And she's not shy."

Hillary snickered. "That's for sure."

I turned onto the gravel driveway that led up to Sandy's house. But Hillary held me back. "Wait," she murmured, gazing up at the house.

"What's wrong?" I asked, turning and studying her face.

"Al has been pestering me again," Hillary said, rolling her eyes. "Do you believe it?"

"What does he want this time?" I asked. "More money?"

Hillary shook her head. "He made me lend him my car."

"Oh wow," I murmured.

"I—I've been so upset and angry about Al, I just had to tell someone," Hillary stammered.

"Well, of course you can tell me," I replied. "I'm your best friend."

"He's always after me for money, or for my history notes, or for my car," Hillary continued, talking rapidly as always, her voice tight with anger. "He pesters me all the time. And if I try to say no to him—"

"He threatens to tell your parents about the chemistry exam." I finished the sentence for her. "I'm in the same boat, Hillary." I sighed. "He threatens me all the time too."

"I *hate* myself for letting this happen to me!" Hillary wailed. She balled her hands into tight fists. "Al has such power over me and it's all my fault. I never should have taken that old test from him. Never, never, *never*! It's the biggest mistake of my life!"

I stared at my friend in shock. In all the years we'd been friends, I'd never seen her totally lose it like that.

I placed a hand on her shoulder. She was shaking! "It'll be okay," I said softly, soothingly. "He's doing the same thing to me. But he'll get bored. Really."

Her dark eyes locked on mine. "Bored? Do you think so?"

I nodded. "Al has a very short attention span. He'll get tired of bullying us. He'll move on to some new victims. You'll see."

She didn't reply. I could see she was thinking hard, maybe about what I'd just said.

We made our way up the driveway, our shoes crunching noisily over the gravel. I raised my finger to the doorbell, but the front door swung open before I could press it.

Sandy pushed open the glass storm door. I could see instantly from the troubled expression on his face that something was wrong.

"Sandy—what is it?" I said.

"Did you hear about Al?" Sandy asked.

4

uh?" I uttered. A hard shudder ran down my body. I could feel the back of my neck tighten.

"Come in. Hurry," Sandy urged. He held open the door, and Hillary and I slid past him into the living room. Taylor and Vincent were sitting at opposite ends of the green leather couch. Despite the blustery weather, Taylor wore khaki shorts and a pink midriff top that left most of her stomach bare.

I nodded to them both. "What about Al?" I said, turning to Sandy.

"He got suspended from school." Taylor answered the question for Sandy.

"Yeah, he did." Sandy nodded, shaking his head. He nibbled his bottom lip. He looks a lot younger when he does that.

Sandy is short and a little chubby. He has a

nice face—nothing special, but nice. But he always reminds me of a shy, fretful twelve-year-old.

"Why?" Hillary demanded. "Why'd they suspend him?"

Vincent grinned at us. "Al rolled up his English term paper and smoked it in front of Mrs. Hirsch."

Hillary and I both gasped.

"You're kidding!" I cried.

Vincent's grin grew wider. "Yeah. I'm kidding. He got into a fight."

"Can't you ever be serious?" Sandy asked Vincent sharply.

Vincent shook his head.

Taylor reached across the couch and slapped Vincent's shoulder. "You're terrible!" she declared.

"Thanks," Vincent replied.

I think Vincent has an adorable grin. His whole face crinkles up. He has awesome gray-green eyes that always seem to be laughing. He has rust-colored hair that he parts in the middle. It nearly comes down to his collar and looks kind of cute.

The rest of him is tall and gangly and gawky, and doesn't go with his face at all. He has big hands and big feet, and he's totally klutzy.

He's sort of a big, clumsy clown. Only cute. I'm basically nuts about him. But I've mentioned that.

And I sometimes wish, along with Sandy and

the others, that Vincent wouldn't clown around *all* the time. After all, if Al really did get suspended from school, it could mess up his entire life.

"Al got into a fight with David Arnold," Sandy explained excitedly. "After school. In the hallway outside the gym."

"But isn't David on the wrestling team?" I asked.

"Yeah. That's who Al decides to pick on. One of the biggest guys in school. Smart, huh?" Sandy said.

"He should've picked on some shrimp—like you!" Vincent teased Sandy.

Sandy growled at him.

"Stop kidding around. What happened?" I demanded impatiently.

Vincent laughed. "Al punched David several times with his face!"

"That's not funny," Sandy snapped at Vincent.

"It's kind of funny," Hillary chimed in. I was surprised to see her grinning. After all, Al used to be a good friend of ours. But I guess I shouldn't have been surprised. Not the way Al had been bullying Hillary.

"They wrestled around, that's all," Sandy continued. "Al got hurt a lot worse than David. And then when Al finally threw a punch, guess who came around the corner just in time to see it?"

"Mr. Hernandez?" I guessed.

Sandy nodded. "Yeah. The principal. So Al got suspended and David didn't. Al's parents are probably on their way to school right now."

"Are they going to be steamed, or what?" Vincent demanded.

"Wow," I murmured. I dropped into the green leather armchair opposite the couch. "Wow."

"You can repeat that for me," Hillary said. She had been standing with her backpack on. Now she tossed it against the side of the couch.

Taylor stood up and stretched. She rubbed her stomach under the short pink midriff top.

When did she have time to go home and change from her school clothes? I wondered. *And why is she dressed for summertime? Just showing off?*

"I can't believe Al used to be part of your group," Taylor said, her eyes on Sandy. "I mean, he's such a loser. He's so messed up."

"Yeah. He's messing up his whole life," Sandy agreed.

"Hey," Vincent said, grinning as usual, "if you've only got one life to mess up, it might as well be your own!"

Taylor rubbed her stomach again. "I'm starving," she complained. "Is there anything to eat?"

"Sure! No problem!" Sandy cried.

Hillary and I exchanged glances. Hillary was right. Sandy jumped at Taylor's every command.

"I think I saw a bag of those black tortilla chips," Sandy told her. "And there might be a jar of salsa in the refrigerator."

"Did you know that people in the United States buy more salsa than ketchup?" Vincent announced.

We all ignored him. Vincent is always spouting these bizarre facts. They're usually true—but who cares?

We followed Sandy into the kitchen. Taylor spotted the bag of tortilla chips on the counter. She tore it open, grabbed a handful, and began downing them eagerly.

Hillary watched Taylor grab a second handful of chips and devour them hungrily. "How do you stay so skinny if you eat all those tortilla chips?" Hillary demanded.

Taylor didn't miss a beat. "I try to throw up every night," she replied.

We all laughed. Sometimes Taylor really cracks us up.

Sandy, meanwhile, was struggling with the glass jar of salsa. He strained and groaned, trying to twist the lid off. He turned the jar upside down and pounded it on the countertop.

No go.

He kept glancing at Taylor. I think he was embarrassed that he wasn't strong enough to pull off the lid. Guys are weird that way.

"Let me try it," Hillary offered. Sandy started to protest. But she pulled the jar from his hands.

She twisted the top off without any effort at all. She grinned triumphantly at Sandy. "Superwoman!"

Sandy blushed. He shouldn't have been embarrassed by a dumb thing like that. But I saw that he really felt humiliated.

"I loosened it up for you," he grumbled.

Hillary crooked her arm and made her bicep bulge. "I'm in great shape. I work out every morning," she bragged.

"She does tongue push-ups!" Vincent joked.

"Ha-ha," Hillary replied sarcastically. She dipped a chip into the jar, then passed the jar to Taylor.

"You guys should come down to my basement," Hillary said. "My dad bought all kinds of workout equipment. I do about half an hour every morning before school. I'll bet I'm in better shape than any guy at Shadyside High."

That's so typical of Hillary, I thought. She always has to be the best at everything.

Sandy started to say something. But he was

interrupted by a loud pounding at the kitchen door.

We all turned to the window at the same time.

When I saw Al on the back stoop, I felt cold dread tighten my stomach.

What does he want? I wondered.

And why does he look so weird?

5

Sandy started to the door.

"I—I don't think you should let him in," Hillary warned Sandy.

Al pounded on the glass with his big fist, so hard I gritted my teeth, waiting for the window to shatter. "Hey, guys!" he shouted. "Hey, guys—it's me!"

Sandy hesitated with his hand on the doorknob. "Why is he yelling like that?"

"I think he's drunk or something," Taylor said, stepping up behind Sandy.

"Well, we *have* to let him in," Vincent piped up. "He's staring right at us. He'll pound on the door all day. We can't just pretend he's invisible."

"Hey, guys! Open up! Hey, you ugly creeps! Yo—it's me!" Al drove his shoulder into the door.

"Oh!" Hillary uttered a frightened cry.

"I've got to let him in," Sandy groaned. "The big moron is going to break down the door."

Sandy turned the lock and pulled open the kitchen door.

Al stumbled into the kitchen, his eyes wild. "Why didn't you open up?" He spoke slowly, his eyes rolling from one of us to the next.

"We didn't hear you," Sandy told him.

Pretty lame.

"Huh?" Al rocked unsteadily, as if he was having trouble keeping his balance. He squinted at Sandy.

"He's totaled," I whispered to Hillary. "He's really drunk."

"As a skunk," Hillary whispered back.

Al pushed past Sandy and lurched toward the refrigerator on rubbery legs. "Got any beer in there?" He pulled open the door.

"Hey—no way," Sandy cried, moving quickly to stop Al.

Al spun around—and nearly fell over. "No beer? I saw a sissspack on the bottom sssshelf."

"No. Sorry," Sandy said tensely. He tried to push the refrigerator door shut. But Al hung on to it.

Sandy glanced nervously at Taylor. Then he turned back to Al. He put a hand on Al's shoulder. "Sit down, okay?"

Al angrily swiped Sandy's hand away. "Get off me, man," he muttered, lowering his voice menacingly. He glared at Sandy with watery eyes. "Get off me. Don't touch me."

"Take it easy, Al," I chimed in, rushing up beside Sandy. "We heard what happened at school. We feel bad for you. You got a bad deal."

I don't think Al heard a word I said. He stood in the square of light from the open refrigerator, glaring angrily at Sandy. Despite the coolness of the day, his forehead dripped with sweat.

Taylor and Vincent hung back, standing awkwardly in front of the kitchen table. Hillary stood in the middle of the room, arms crossed over her chest, her face expressionless, eyes not blinking, locked on Al.

Sandy tried again to tug Al from the refrigerator. But Al ducked his big shoulder and bumped Sandy off.

"I don't like the way you're looking at me, man," Al said angrily.

"Al, please—" Sandy pleaded.

"Like you're better than me," Al muttered nastily.

Sandy took a step back. He is at least a foot shorter than Al, and not at all athletic.

"Like you're better than me," Al repeated.

"Think you're better than me, Sandy? Think you're some kind of cool dude or something?"

"Al, please close the refrigerator and come sit down," Sandy insisted, motioning to the kitchen table.

"We didn't do anything to you," I added, trying to distract him from Sandy. "We're your friends."

He kept his eyes focused on Sandy. "Think you're better than me? Think you're sssso hot because Taylor pretends to like you?"

"Al, shut up!" Taylor cried shrilly from behind us.

"Yeah—shut up," Hillary growled in a cold, tense voice.

"You're a fat little wimp," Al sneered at Sandy.

Sandy's face reddened. I saw the veins throb in his neck.

Al giggled. I have no idea what struck him as funny. "Fat little wimp," he repeated, whispering this time.

Challenging Sandy. Daring him to do something.

"Hey, Al—haven't you been in enough fights for one day?" Vincent called out.

"Please close the refrigerator door," Sandy requested again, his jaw clenched, his face still red.

Al grinned at him, an ugly, unpleasant grin. "Make me."

"Sandy—no!" I cried. Too late.

Sandy reached for Al's arm. Grabbed him just above the wrist. Gave him a hard tug away from the refrigerator.

Al shouted a curse—and swung his other fist.

Al swayed, off-balance. But his fist made a sickening *thock* against the side of Sandy's face.

Sandy uttered a sharp cry. He stumbled back, and his hand shot up to his cheek.

Breathing hard, sweat pouring down his face, Al leaned heavily against the refrigerator door. Eyes wide, locked on Sandy. Watching to see if Sandy would hit him back.

Bright red blood trickled from Sandy's mouth, onto the tile floor. There was now a small cut on his cheek. "My tooth . . ." Sandy spit out more blood. "You knocked out a tooth."

Al rubbed the back of his fist, his eyes on Sandy. Sandy glared back at him, holding his cheek, blood pouring from his open mouth.

I heard an angry cry behind me. Spun around in time to see Hillary dive at Al.

"No—*don't!*" I shrieked. "Hillary—*don't!*"

Hillary slammed Al back hard against the refrigerator.

He grunted in surprise. Then a smile spread quickly over his perspiring face as he grabbed Hillary's arms and pushed her back.

"Okay," he said, breathing hard. "Okay. No problem. I'll fight you, too."

6

Gripping each other by the shoulders, Hillary and Al glared face-to-face, wheezing, gasping for breath.

"I'll fight you. I don't care. I'll fight you," Al chanted. With a burst of strength, he tried to shove Hillary away.

But she was stronger than he thought. She held on to his shoulders. He couldn't budge her.

"I'll fight you. Want to fight? I'll fight you," he threatened. But the wild light faded from his eyes. His whole body appeared to sag.

He let go of Hillary, and his arms dropped to his sides.

He stared at her, standing unsteadily, his chest rising and falling under his sweat-drenched black T-shirt, gulping in mouthfuls of air.

Hillary didn't back up. She stood with her fists

hard at her sides. Her long braid had come apart. Her black hair fell over her face. She made no attempt to brush it away.

Al shrugged his broad shoulders. "Okay, okay. Forget about the beer." He stepped around Hillary. Gave Sandy a hard, two-handed push on the chest that sent Sandy stumbling back. Then he strode to the door, a triumphant sneer on his face.

"Some friends I got," Al muttered. "Can't get a lousy beer." He cursed at us and banged the door on his way out.

As the door slammed, Taylor and Vincent rushed forward to help Sandy. "I'll get some water. A cold washcloth," Taylor offered. She disappeared toward the bathroom.

Vincent led Sandy to a kitchen chair. "You'll have to see someone about that tooth. But the cut isn't too deep," Vincent assured him. "It shouldn't mess up your beautiful face."

That's right, Vincent, I thought. *Keep it light.*

I started to feel a little calmer. My hands were still as cold as ice. But at least my heart had stopped pounding like a bass drum.

I turned back to Hillary—and froze.

She hadn't moved from in front of the refrigerator. She stood so stiffly, her hands were still clenched into fists. Her entire body was clenched.

She was staring straight ahead, staring at nothing. And she was biting her bottom lip, biting it so hard it bled.

"Hillary . . . ?" I whispered.

She didn't hear me. She seemed to be in some kind of a trance.

"Hillary . . . ?"

Watching her, I felt a chill run down my back. I realized I had never seen so much hatred on her face before. I had never seen so much hatred on *anyone's* face!

Just how hard a time has Al been giving Hillary? I found myself wondering.

Just how much does she hate him?

I didn't see Al for several days after that horrible afternoon. But I heard from some friends of his that he was suspended from school for two weeks.

It's a terrible thing to admit, but I felt glad that he couldn't come to school. It meant I didn't have to be afraid of him trapping me in the hall, demanding lunch money or my history notes or something.

Hillary and I didn't talk about it. But I'm sure she felt the same way.

On Thursday, I was supposed to meet Vincent at his house after school. We were doing a chemistry lab project together.

I hoped maybe it would help get a special chemistry going between *us*! Ha-ha.

Anyway, I got hung up, talking to Corky Corcoran and some of the cheerleaders about helping out with their spring car wash. So I didn't get to Vincent's house until after four thirty.

It was a warm, humid day, and I jogged most of the way. To my surprise, I found Vincent out on his driveway, pacing nervously up and down.

"Sorry I'm late!" I called, brushing back my hair. I felt something kind of dry and flaky caught in my hair. I pulled it out and examined it. A huge, gray moth.

Nothing like looking your best when you're with a guy you have a crush on!

Vincent growled a greeting. He stared past me to the street.

I thought maybe he would notice the sexy new spring outfit I was wearing. A short, blue, pleated miniskirt from the sixties and a blue-and-black-striped sleeveless top. I bought it at a new store at the mall called Street Grunge. And I saved it until a time I knew I'd be alone with Vincent.

But of course he didn't even look at me.

"What's your problem?" I demanded. "What are you doing out here, anyway? I thought maybe you'd start the experiments."

"Huh? You want me to do all the work?"

Grumpy, grumpy. This wasn't like Vincent at all. What happened to Mr. Funnyman?

"Well, why are you out here?" I persisted. "Just getting some fresh air?"

"I wish," he muttered bitterly. "I'm waiting for Al. He's late."

"Al?" I couldn't hide my surprise.

"Yeah. That big creep Al." Vincent scowled and kicked a small rock across the driveway.

I pulled the backpack off my shoulder and tossed it to the grass. Then I straightened my new top over the skirt. "You're waiting for Al out here?"

Vincent nodded glumly. "He took my mom's car."

I gasped "He *stole* it?"

"No. I loaned it to him," Vincent replied, shaking his head. "I mean, he *forced* me to loan it to him."

"Oh wow," I murmured, swallowing hard. Big Al strikes again.

"He promised he'd bring it back an hour ago," Vincent moaned. "He said he'd have it back here by the time I got home from school."

He turned his gray-green eyes to the street and searched in both directions. A warm breeze fluttered his rust-colored hair. He looked so adorable. I had a sudden impulse to kiss him and tell him everything would be okay.

How do you think *that* would go over?

"If my parents find out I loaned that jerk their car, they will *murder* me!" Vincent exclaimed. "No lie. They will murder me."

"So why did you let him take it?" I asked softly.

Vincent scowled again. He was always so mellow. It really upset me to see him so stressed.

"I did a stupid thing," he confessed. "I took my parents' car Saturday night without telling them. They were down the street at a party. I just felt like getting out. You know. Spring fever or something. So I took the car and cruised around town for a while.

"I guess I was going too fast or something," Vincent continued, his eyes on the street. "I was two blocks from home. I got pulled over by a cop. I got a fifty-dollar speeding ticket. Do you believe it? And who comes walking up while I'm getting the ticket? Yeah. You guessed it. The Man. Al."

"Bad news," I murmured.

"The cop drove off," Vincent continued. "I told Al he'd never see me again because my parents would definitely murder me. I mean, I took the car without asking. Then I got the ticket for a big five-oh. I was dead meat."

A high cloud rolled over the sun. A blue shadow swept over the front lawn.

Vincent's expression darkened too. "So Al says no big deal. He'll help me. My parents will never know."

"What did he do?" I asked.

Vincent shook his head. "He took the speeding ticket and ripped it into tiny shreds. He said the police computers never work. My parents will never find out about the ticket."

"Big help," I muttered.

"Well, maybe he's right," Vincent argued. "But then he came over here yesterday and made me promise to lend him Mom's car today. He said he only needed it for two hours. He said if I didn't let him have the car, he'd tell my parents I sneaked out Saturday night and tore up a speeding ticket."

"He's doing it to you, too," I said.

"What choice did I have?" Vincent moaned. "I let him take the car. But where is he? Mom's office car pool gets her home a little after five. If the car isn't back by then . . ."

"He'll be here," I said. But I didn't sound real convincing.

I didn't trust Al. Why should I?

Vincent and I both turned to the street and watched. I tried talking about our chem experiments. But Vincent couldn't concentrate on anything but waiting. We both kept glancing at our watches, watching the time slip quickly toward five.

And then at about five till five, we heard a rattling sound from down the street. A clatter of metal against metal.

I recognized Al as he turned the car into the driveway.

Vincent gasped. His jaw dropped nearly to the ground.

"Oh noooo!" he wailed. "I don't believe it!"

7

"Hey, it wasn't my fault, man!" Al cried, sticking his head out the driver's window.

He pulled the car to a stop in front of Vincent and me.

The front of the car was just about totaled. The left front fender was crushed in. The hood was mangled. One end of the bumper dragged on the ground.

Vincent didn't say a word. I think he was in shock. His mouth hung wide open and he kept swallowing noisily.

I put a hand on his shoulder. I wanted to say something comforting, something hopeful. But I couldn't think of anything.

Vincent moved slowly from one side of the car to the other, his eyes locked on the smashed-in hood and fender, the sagging bumper. He was so upset, I don't think he even knew that I was standing beside him.

"Really. It wasn't my fault," Al repeated out the open window. He climbed out of the car, wearing black as usual. A black baseball cap covered his blond hair.

The driver's door made a loud *squawk* as he pushed it open. I saw that the door was banged in too.

"N-not your fault?" Vincent stammered in a choked voice.

"I couldn't see the stop sign," Al explained. "There were tree leaves in front of it. Really, man. How could I know it was there? It wasn't my fault."

Vincent let out a long moan. He stared at the mangled car, shaking his head.

A grin spread across Al's face. "At least I got it back on time!"

And that's when Vincent lost it.

He leaped onto Al like some kind of wild jungle animal. Growling and scratching and screaming and cursing and tearing at him.

I froze for a second. Startled. Frightened.

Then I shot across the driveway. Grabbed Vincent from behind. Swept my arms around his waist. And pulled.

"Stop it, Vincent! Stop it!" I shrieked.

I pulled him off Al. But he was still swearing and swinging his fists, bellowing like a furious lion.

"Let go of me, Julie! Let me go!" Vincent struggled to free himself.

"Vincent—please! *Please!*" I pleaded.

Al had fallen back against the car. I saw him pulling himself up. He straightened his black T-shirt. Picked up his cap from the driveway. I saw his little blue eyes narrow menacingly. Saw his face tighten in anger.

"Let me go!" Vincent screamed.

I held on tight. "No, Vincent. No way! He'll only pound you," I insisted. "You know I'm right. You can't fight him. He'll pound you!"

"But he can't keep getting away with this stuff!" Vincent cried. "He can't!"

I glanced up.

To my surprise, Al had turned away and was jogging down the driveway. Without calling to us, without uttering a word, he turned at the sidewalk and disappeared, jogging, behind a tall hedge.

Al never looked back.

That was on Thursday.

The next night—Friday night—I killed him.

PART 2

8

Well . . . some people thought I killed Al.

But of course I didn't.

After dinner on Friday, I called Vincent. He greeted me with a glum hello. Even over the phone, I could tell that he was upset and very depressed.

I tried to cheer him up. "We're all going blading at the Shadyside Rink," I told him. "Want to come?"

Vincent is a terror on Rollerblades! He whirls around wildly and waves his arms like a crazy person. He always skates about five times faster than everyone else. Which is bad news because he's a *terrible* skater!

I can't tell you how many times we've had to scrape him off the wall or pull him up off the floor, mangled and dazed. He just can't ever do anything seriously. He always has to be funny—even when he risks trashing himself for good!

"I can't go," Vincent moaned. "I can't go any-where, Julie. I'm grounded. I think, forever."

"Oh no," I murmured. "Because of the car?"

"Yeah. Because of the car," Vincent repeated unhappily. "I'm grounded forever. I'll never see you guys again." He sighed. "And that's not the worst part."

I took a deep breath. "What's the worst part?"

"I can't take that job as a camp counselor this summer," Vincent replied. His voice cracked. I knew he really wanted the camp job.

"I have to stay in Shadyside all summer and work in my dad's shop." Vincent groaned. "It's to help pay for the car damage."

"You mean you don't get to keep the money you earn?" I asked.

"No, I don't." His voice was so low, I had to press the phone against my ear to hear him. "No. It all goes to my dad to pay for what that creep Al did to the car."

"Oh wow," I murmured.

I felt so bad for Vincent. He didn't total the car. Al did. Vincent didn't even want to lend Al the car.

"Al should pay for the car," I said.

Vincent let out a dry, bitter laugh. "*You* go tell that to Al."

A long silence. I could hear Vincent breathing on the other end. I tried to think of something cheerful to say.

I was worried about him. I really was. This was the first time I'd ever talked with him when he didn't crack a single joke. I felt as if his whole personality had changed. He sounded so totally down, so totally depressed.

All because of that big jerk Al.

"Can I come over to your house?" I suggested. "I'll forget about going blading. We could just hang out."

"Not allowed," he answered glumly. "I can't go anywhere, and I'm not allowed to have visitors. I'm a prisoner. A total prisoner."

"Well, maybe—" I started. But I could hear his father yelling at him in the background.

"Okay, okay! Give me a break! I'm getting off!" Vincent shouted angrily to his dad. He returned to me. "Got to go. Tell everyone hi." And he hung up.

I put the phone down and paced back and forth in my room for a short while. *Vincent's parents will get over it,* I decided. *They'll calm down. They'll let Vincent go back to his normal life.*

A long blast from a car horn snapped me from my thoughts. I peered out the window to the driveway and saw Hillary's blue Jetta.

I gave my hair a quick brush, grabbed my

Rollerblades, and hurried down to the car. "Hey, guys." I slid into the front passenger seat. Taylor and Sandy were in the back seat, pressed together, her white-blond hair falling onto his shoulder. I glimpsed her sleeveless top and the short blue skirt she wore over dark tights.

"Is Vincent coming?" Hillary asked, backing down the drive.

"Vincent isn't going anywhere," I reported. I told them the whole story.

When I finished, Hillary and Taylor both burst out in angry attacks on Al, both protested how unfair Vincent's parents were being. Sandy remained strangely quiet.

The rink was really crowded, even for a Friday night. I saw a lot of kids from our high school and a lot of younger kids. There aren't that many places to go in Shadyside. The skating rink is one of the few places to hang out with your friends.

During the winter, the floor is covered with ice, and we all come here to ice skate and sit around, drinking cups and cups of coffee and hot chocolate. The ice had been removed only two weeks ago. So a lot of kids were eager to try out their new Rollerblades.

The four of us sat on the long bench outside the skating area. We took our time lacing up our skates. Taylor had trouble getting her laces tight enough. So Sandy got down on his knees and fixed them for her.

It struck me funny. Sandy was so desperate to please. He didn't mind being Taylor's slave.

I knew Vincent would have made a joke about it. He would have given Sandy a really hard time and made us all laugh.

So far, we weren't laughing very much. I think the others felt as bad about Vincent as I did. Al was messing up *all* our lives. And there wasn't much we could do about it.

I brushed my hair back over my shoulders and rolled onto the rink. I decided to try to forget about Al and Vincent and everything, and just have a good time.

I'm a pretty good skater. I've got strong ankles. And I love blading, even around in circles in a rink.

But I was a little rusty. I mean, I hadn't bladed since last fall. And the rink was so jammed with kids.

I made a few circles, gliding unsteadily. I guess I picked up a little more speed than I was ready for.

"Whooa!" I cried out as I spun too hard in a turn—and bumped hard into a skinny, red-haired boy. His hands shot up. He cried out angrily.

And we both fell. I landed on top of him. Heard his grunt of surprise and pain.

"Sorry," I uttered breathlessly. Did I *crush* the little guy?

I scrambled to my feet. Bent to help him up. And recognized him.

Artie Matthews. One of the twins I used to babysit for.

Sure enough, Chucky, his brother, came rolling over. He slid to a stop, his blue eyes narrowed first at his twin, then at me.

In an instant, I remembered how much I *hated* these two boys. *They must be about twelve now,* I realized. I used to babysit them when they were nine.

They looked like angels, but they weren't.

As soon as their parents were out the door, they went wild. Fighting each other. Torturing the dog. Trashing the house. Refusing to go to bed.

"Are you okay?" I asked Artie.

"Why don't you watch where you're going?" he snarled at me, rubbing his elbow.

"Julie—what are *you* doing here?" Chucky demanded. "Aren't you too old to be on Rollerblades?"

They both burst into high-pitched giggles at that. Ha-ha.

I made sure that Artie wasn't injured. Then I skated over to join Hillary.

"Take some lessons!" I heard Artie call after me. And I heard their obnoxious giggles again.

"Didn't you used to babysit for those twins?" Hillary asked as I skated up beside her.

I nodded. "I just fell on one of them," I told her. "But not hard enough!"

I waved to some girls from school, keeping in a steady rhythm with Hillary. "Where are Sandy and Taylor?" I asked, my eyes making a circle, searching the crowd.

Hillary pointed.

They hadn't left the bench. They were wrapped around each other like two octopuses. Taylor was practically on his lap. Her blond hair fell over his face as she kissed him.

I stared at them for a long moment, and nearly skated into the wall!

"Maybe she really *does* like him," Hillary said wistfully.

"Maybe," I replied.

A short while later, Taylor and Sandy disappeared together. I'm not sure why they bothered to bring their skates.

Hillary and I bladed for about twenty minutes. We ran into some kids we knew, and we hung out with them at the food stand for a while.

Then Hillary saw a guy from Waynesbridge she knew. Waving and shouting his name, she hurried over to talk to him.

I tightened my skate laces, preparing to skate some more. The muscles throbbed. It felt good. I needed the exercise. I hadn't done anything athletic all winter.

"Hey, listen." I felt Hillary's hand on my shoulder. "John and I are going to a party he knows about." She pointed to the kid from Waynesbridge, a tall, thin guy wearing a loose-fitting red shirt over huge, baggy jeans. "Want to come? You're welcome to come with us."

I shook my head. "No. Go ahead. I want to skate some more."

She brought her face close to mine and stared into my eyes. "You sure you don't mind me deserting you like this?"

"Hillary, it's no problem," I assured her. "I really want to get some exercise. I'll get a ride home with someone. Or else I'll take the bus."

I watched her hurry away with John. Then I rolled onto the rink, holding the rail. I wished Vincent had been able to come. I didn't mind everyone leaving. I just wished Vincent were there.

Anyway, I bladed for about half an hour. I enjoyed it. It felt really good to give my legs a workout. And the rink has an awesome sound system and plays really great music.

I guess it was about eleven o'clock when I

decided to leave. I couldn't find anyone to give me a ride. So I counted out my change for the bus. It didn't run very often this late at night, but maybe I'd get lucky.

I jammed my Rollerblades into the carrying bag and made my way out the back exit of the rink. There's a narrow alley back there, a shortcut to the bus stop.

I stepped into the alley. The air felt surprisingly cool. I guess I was overheated from skating. My legs tingled. I gazed up at a small crescent moon hanging between the buildings. A single yellow light bulb cast a pale cone of light over the alley.

I could hear voices from the street beyond the alley. I heard the screech of car tires. I could hear the steady drumbeat from the sound system in the skating rink behind me.

I took five or six steps into the alley—then stopped.

I recognized Al's face.

That's the first thing I saw. His face.

It made me stop and raise my hands to my cheeks.

Al's face.

Why was he lying on his back in the alley?

I saw his legs sprawled on the concrete, one knee raised.

I saw his hands angled from his sides, balled into tight fists.

And then I saw the skates.

The laces around his throat. The laces stretched so tight around his throat that his eyes bulged.

His eyes bulged, staring lifelessly up at the crescent moon.

His face pale, so ghostly pale in the dim alley light.

The laces so tight, twisted around and around his throat, cutting into his neck.

And one skate — the front of the skate — jammed into his mouth. Jammed so tight, it stood up in his mouth.

Al. Dead in the alley. Strangled by the skates. Strangled and smothered.

And dead.

9

"Ohhhh." I uttered a low moan. More of an animal cry than a human sound.

The skate bag fell from my hand. My legs were shaking so hard, I dropped to my knees.

And knelt over Al.

Knelt over Al's body—and stared. I realized I had never seen a dead body before.

It's so weird, the thoughts that flash through your mind when you're gripped in shock, in horror. But that's what I thought, leaning over Al, staring down at him: *I've never seen a dead body before.*

I stared at his eyes. They reflected the crescent moon. Like glass. Glass eyes. Doll eyes. No longer real.

I stared at the skate. The toe of the boot crammed so deep into his open mouth. The wheels glowing dully in the yellow alley light.

The other skate lay under Al's head. The two skates were tied together. The laces that connected them were wrapped around Al's neck.

Wrapped so tight. So tight.

My stomach lurched. I held my breath. Struggled to keep my dinner down.

Without thinking, I reached one hand out.

What did I plan to do? Touch the skate jammed into Al's mouth? Pull it out?

I'm not sure. I wasn't thinking at all. I mean, all sorts of wild thoughts were flooding my mind. But I wasn't thinking clearly. I wasn't thinking or making a plan or deciding what I should do or where I should go or who I should call—or anything!

I leaned over Al's body.

He's no longer Al, I thought.

He's not Al. Now he's Al's body.

I reached out. Started to touch the heel of the skate.

But a burst of sound made me pull my hand back.

I heard the thunder of drums, an explosion of guitars.

The back door to the rink opened.

I heard footsteps. And then a scream.

"He's *dead*!" someone squealed. A high, shrill voice. I didn't recognize it at first.

"He's dead!"

And then another shrill voice. "She *killed* him!"

"Noooo!" I screamed. I spun around. Off-balance. Dizzy.

I turned to the high-pitched voices. And in the shadows outside the yellow alley light, I saw Artie and Chucky.

Their red hair glowing dully, rising like flames over their pale faces. Their blue eyes wide with fear.

"She *killed* him!"

"No—wait!" I pleaded, stumbling, staggering to my feet. My legs so rubbery, shaking so hard. "Wait—!"

"She killed him! I saw her!"

"Call the police!"

"No—please!" I started after them. "Artie! Chucky—no!"

Another explosion of music as they pushed the door open. And disappeared back into the rink.

Leaving the image of their startled eyes glowing in my mind.

Leaving their shrill cries of horror in my ears.

"No—wait! I didn't! I didn't!" My panicked

cries falling unheard to the concrete alley ground. "You're wrong! You're wrong! Wait—you're wrong!"

I didn't do it, I told myself. I didn't. I didn't.

The police will believe me, I decided.

I know they will.

10

W e believe you," Officer Reed said softly, leaning over his cluttered desk. He was a big bear
of a man, with a red, round face and bushy
gray eyebrows over small, round, bloodshot eyes.
The glare of the overhead light reflected off his bald
head. The collar of his blue uniform shirt was open.
He pulled off his navy blue tie and tossed it onto
the desk.

"We believe you. But we have to ask a lot of
upsetting questions anyway." He narrowed his eyes
at me. "Do you understand, Julie?"

I nodded and glanced at my parents. They
sat huddled close together on the other side of the
policeman's desk. Mom kept dabbing at tears in
her eyes with a balled-up tissue. Dad had one arm
around her shoulders as if holding her down.

"I know we've been over everything twice

before. But I need to go over it one more time,"
Officer Reed said wearily. He mopped sweat off his
bald head and forehead with the palm of his hand.
"You see, it just doesn't add up. It doesn't make
sense to me."

"But I told you everything! What part doesn't
make sense?" I demanded. I clasped my hands
tightly in my lap to keep them from shaking.

Mom held my skate bag on her lap, shifting it
from leg to leg. I wondered why she didn't put it
down on the floor.

Even when you're being questioned by the
police about a murder, your mind wanders. I found
myself thinking about Hillary. Wondering if she was
enjoying the party.

I tried to imagine how she would react when
she heard about Al later tonight.

Officer Reed rubbed his jaw. "What you told
me makes sense, Julie. You came out of the skating
rink and found the body in the alley. It's the *murder*
that doesn't make sense."

I stared at him, swallowing hard. My mouth
felt so dry. I took a long sip of water from the
paper cup he had placed on the corner of his
desk for me. The water was warm and tasted kind
of sour. Or maybe that was just the taste in my
mouth.

"For one thing, he wasn't robbed," Officer Reed continued. "He still had his wallet with about fifteen dollars in it." He raised his bloodshot eyes to me. "He didn't usually carry around large sums of money, did he?"

"No," I replied. "Al was usually broke. He was always trying to borrow money from me."

My parents both stared at me. I was sorry I said it. I didn't want them to start asking a lot of questions about why I loaned money to Al.

Officer Reed rubbed his jaw again. "He wasn't robbed. So why was he murdered?"

"I don't know," I started. "I don't think—"

"And why was he murdered in such a brutal way?" the policeman continued, looking over my shoulder at the pale yellow wall behind me. "It almost looks as if someone was showing off. Or maybe showing Al something. You know. Paying him back for something. Teaching him a lesson."

"Some lesson," my dad muttered. Mom let out a whimpering cry and dabbed at her eyes.

"I'm okay, Mom. Really," I whispered to her.

"I just can't believe you had to see something so . . . horrible," Mom replied.

The policeman didn't seem to hear her. He stared at the wall, deep in his own thoughts.

A heavy silence fell over the small office as I

waited for him to say something. I took another sip of the warm water.

What is he thinking? I wondered. *What does he think happened?*

At least he believed my story, I thought with relief. At least he didn't believe those stupid twins. He knows I'm not a murderer.

Someone is.

The thought forced its way into my mind, making me shudder.

Someone is a murderer.

Officer Reed cleared his throat. He leaned over the desk, elbows brushing stacks of paper aside. "So we have to ask ourselves about a motive," he said. "Why did someone kill a teenage boy so brutally if not for money?"

He tapped his stubby fingers on the desktop, staring hard at me the whole while. "Julie—any ideas? Do you know anyone who might not like Al? Anyone who might have something against him? Something serious against him?"

"Well . . ." I took a deep breath.

What should I say? How honest should I be?

Should I tell him how much we all hated Al? Should I tell him how Al bullied us and blackmailed us and threatened us?

"I'll need a list of his friends," the police officer

interrupted, frowning. "Do you know his friends? I believe you said he used to be part of your group?"

I nodded. "But not this year," I told him. "Al got some new friends. Guys we didn't like. From Waynesbridge. Sort of tough kids. He—"

"Tough kids?" Officer Reed's eyes suddenly flashed with interest. "He started hanging out with a group of tough kids? Do you know them, Julie? Do you think any of them might have a motive for killing Al?"

"I—I don't know," I stammered. "I don't think—"

He raised a big paw to quiet me. "Think hard. Take a deep breath. Think for a minute. Anything Al ever said to you about his friends? Any comment he made about someone being angry or annoyed at him?"

"We *all* were!" I blurted out.

The words escaped my mouth in a rush. I hadn't meant to say them. They just exploded from me. I couldn't hold them in any longer.

I heard my mother gasp. The skate bag toppled from her lap.

Officer Reed stopped drumming his fingers on the desk.

"We *all* hated Al!" I cried. Once the dam had burst, the words just kept flowing. I couldn't stop myself if I wanted to.

"All of my friends hated him!" I told the startled policeman. "We all had reasons to hate him. All of us. Me too!"

I took a deep breath. My heart pounded in my chest. "But we didn't do it!" I yelled. "My friends and I—we didn't kill Al. We're just teenagers. We're not murderers!"

That's the truth, I told myself, watching Officer Reed's surprised expression.

We're not murderers. We're not.

That's the truth.

Isn't it?

Isn't it?

11

The weather was all wrong for Al's funeral. Sunny and beautiful, with a warm spring breeze carrying the scent of cherry blossoms.

My first funeral, I thought. *It should be gloomy out, foggy with a cold drizzle of rain.*

Mom didn't want me to go to the funeral. She was trying to protect me. I'm not sure from what.

I told her that Hillary, Sandy, and all my friends planned to be there. So there was no way I could stay home.

True, I kept having nightmares about Al.

Who wouldn't have nightmares after finding a friend strangled in an alley with a skate shoved down his throat?

But I didn't think that going to the funeral would add to my horror—or my nightmares. In a way, the funeral might close this sad and frightening chapter of my life.

At least, that's what I hoped.

As I dressed for the church, pulling on my dark skirt and buttoning my black linen blouse, I had no idea that the horror was just beginning.

I rode with my parents to the church. Mom and Dad didn't know Al's family that well. But they felt they should attend the funeral since Al had been my friend.

No one said a word the whole way. Dad kept his eyes straight ahead on the road. I stared out the window, watching the blur of green from the new leaves on the trees. Thinking about what a beautiful day it was, and how strange it felt to be going to a funeral on such a sunny, cheery day.

The church stood on a low hill outside of town, where Division Street meets the highway. A small, white church. A brass bell in the steeple glowed brightly, reflecting the sunlight.

Large pots of white lilies at the door made the air smell sweet as we stepped inside. Most of the long, dark-wood pews were already filled. I recognized a lot of kids from school and a few teachers.

Mom and Dad slid into seats near the back. I walked down the aisle to talk to Hillary and some other kids. They were clustered near the front, somber expressions on their faces, talking in low tones over the organ music.

Everyone was so dressed up. The boys looked stiff and awkward in their ties and dark blazers. It was all so unreal, like a scene in a movie.

That's what I remember about the funeral.

The boys so uncomfortable in ties and jackets. The soft, unnatural whispers, barely loud enough to be heard over the mournful, depressing organ music.

The smell of lilies. So sweet, it became over-powering.

The cold, damp touch of Hillary's hand as she gripped my arm in greeting.

The long, dark coffin in front of us.

Al couldn't really be lying inside it—could he?

A tiny woman with tight curls of white hair, her head bowed, her lips moving, tears dripping onto the lap of her black dress.

Those are the things I remember.

And the whispered rumors.

Someone said that Al's mother was too over-come to attend the funeral. She had to be sedated and was in the hospital.

Someone said that Al's father had offered a reward to anyone who helped find the killer.

Someone said that the police knew who the

killer was. That it was one of Al's friends from Waynesbridge. He had run off, and the police were searching for him.

Rumors. And the smell of the lilies. And the tiny woman letting her tears fall onto her lap.

I remember all that.

And the faces of my friends.

I had a seat in a side pew. I could see all my friends, their faces pale and drawn and sad. While the minister talked, my eyes moved from one to another.

Sandy leaned forward in the pew, elbows on the bench in front of him, his face buried in his hands. I waited for him to sit back up. But he didn't.

Vincent's features were set and hard. I could see him clenching and unclenching his jaw. He stared straight ahead blankly, as if he were thinking himself somewhere else, somewhere far, far away.

Hillary's face was a blank. I couldn't read it at all. She sat erect, one hand toying with her long, black braid, tugging it, smoothing it. No expression.

Taylor cried softly into a wadded-up tissue. Her white-blond hair had been pinned up on her head. But it had come loose and fell over her face as she dabbed at her eyes.

These aren't the faces of murderers, I thought, watching them, studying them as the minister droned on in front of Al's coffin.

I know these kids.

These are my friends.

Not murderers. Not murderers. Not murderers.

After the funeral, we all met at Sandy's house. Sandy's mom put out plates of sandwiches, which we gobbled up. We were starving!

We all chattered at the same time. We were all tense, I think. Eager to put the funeral behind us. It wasn't easy, since we were still in our funeral clothes.

Vincent pulled off his tie and looped it around his forehead. He seemed a little more like himself. I think he was relieved that his parents allowed him to come to Sandy's house. He'd been grounded for days!

He told us a story about his grandmother's funeral. According to Vincent, she had been a very proper person, very strict, very eager that everything should be done in the right way.

The priest gave a touching eulogy that had everyone in tears, Vincent told us. Then the coffin was opened so that everyone could file past and pay last respects.

But when they opened the coffin, the church filled with horrified gasps. Vincent's grandmother was not inside. Instead everyone stared at an enormous, three-hundred-pound bald man with a bushy Santa Claus beard.

The wrong coffin had been delivered to the church.

The gasps turned to shocked giggles. Then the church echoed with laughter. "People roared," Vincent told us gleefully. "They rolled in the aisles. Really. It was so perfect. My grandmother spent her whole life complaining that no one ever did anything the proper way—and she was *right*!"

We all laughed. Everyone but Sandy. He seemed even more tense than usual. He stood by himself beside the mantel. He had picked up a small bronze bust of himself and was rolling it nervously between his hands.

Sandy's mom is a shrink, but she's also a really talented sculptor. The living room is filled with heads she did of Sandy and Sandy's older sister, Gretchen, who is away at college at Cornell. The likenesses are perfect.

I watched Sandy move the bronze head from hand to hand. He barely listened to Vincent's story. I was surprised that he wasn't paying any attention at all to Taylor.

Taylor and Hillary were talking quietly on the couch. Taylor had pinned her hair back up. Even from across the room, I could see that her eyes were red-rimmed from crying.

"Are you still grounded?" I asked Vincent. "Or did your parents spring you?"

I don't think he heard me. He had his eyes on Taylor. And then he stepped away from me, walking rapidly, and made his way to the kitchen. "Anyone want a Coke or anything?" he called.

I followed him into the kitchen. He had the refrigerator door open and was bending inside. "Are you okay?" I asked.

He pulled out a can of Mountain Dew and stood up. He shrugged. "I guess. It's all pretty weird, isn't it?"

"Yeah. Weird," I agreed.

He popped the top on the can. "Are you okay, Julie? Do you have nightmares or anything? I mean, you're the one who found him there. It must have been . . ."

"I keep picturing it all the time," I confessed. "My parents say it will take a while. They think—"

I stopped when I heard Sandy calling us from the living room. Vincent took a long drink from the soda can. Then we turned and made our way back to the living room to see why Sandy was calling.

"In here," he said. He ushered us into the den. I tried to read his expression. He avoided my gaze. "In here, everyone." His voice sounded tense, hoarse.

"What's this about?" Taylor demanded.

He muttered something, keeping his eyes on

the floor. I couldn't hear him. I don't think Taylor did either.

We all perched around the small, cork-paneled den. Sandy carefully closed the door behind him. "I—I want to tell you something," he said softly. He still held the small, bronze bust of himself between his hands.

"Are you *selling* that thing?" Vincent joked. "Or do you just love yourself?"

Taylor laughed. Hillary and I exchanged glances.

What was Sandy's problem? I wondered. What kind of big announcement did he want to make?

Sandy coughed and cleared his throat. He set the bronze head down on a bookshelf. "I'm only telling you guys this because you're my friends and I trust you," he said, speaking rapidly, his eyes on the window behind my head.

I saw Vincent open his mouth, probably to crack another joke. I shook my head and signaled "no" with my eyes. Vincent dropped back against his chair.

"I want to tell you this, and I don't want to tell you," Sandy said mysteriously. "But I feel that . . . I feel that . . ." His voice trembled. He took a deep breath. "I feel that I have to tell you."

"Sandy—what *is* it?" Taylor cried, jumping to her feet.

"Well . . ." Sandy cleared his throat again. "I—I have a confession to make. You see, I'm the one. I'm the one who killed Al."

12

That's not funny!" I shrieked.

Taylor gasped and drew her hand to her mouth.

Behind her glasses, Hillary narrowed her eyes at Sandy but didn't react.

"You're joking—right?" Vincent demanded, setting down the soda can and climbing to his feet. "What a *sick* joke, man."

Sandy let out a hoarse cry. "It's not a joke, Vincent. I'm not joking. I'm telling you all the truth."

"Noooo!" Taylor shrieked, her eyes wild.

"I did it," Sandy insisted. "I killed Al. You're my friends. I want you to know the truth. I know you will keep my secret."

"Whoa—!" Vincent murmured.

Cold shivers ran down my back. One after the

other. I stared at Sandy. I heard his words. But I didn't believe them.

I didn't *want* to believe them.

"It's not true! It's not true!" Taylor wailed.

She hurtled across the den and threw her arms around Sandy, sobbing. "It's not true! I know it isn't! I know!"

Sandy grabbed her arms and gently pushed her away. "I'm sorry, Taylor. I'm really sorry. But I did it. I'm telling the truth."

Shaking her head, Hillary stood up. She crossed her arms tightly over her chest, walked to the window, and stared out into the afternoon sunlight.

Vincent gaped at Sandy.

I struggled to stop the shivers that shook my body. Finally I found my voice. "But . . . why?" I choked out. "Why, Sandy? What made you do it?"

The room grew quiet. I could hear only Taylor's soft sobs and the rapid pounding of my heart.

"He was ruining our lives," Sandy replied in a low voice just above a whisper. "He was ruining all of our lives. It was getting worse and worse. I—I did it for all of us."

"But, Sandy—" I started.

"We all wanted Al to die, right?" Sandy broke in shrilly. "We all hated him—right? We all hated the way he bullied us, the way he pushed us around, the way he forced us to . . . to . . ." His voice cracked.

"It's not true!" Taylor wailed again. "It's not true! Not true!"

"I'm sorry," Sandy told her softly. "I'm sorry you're so upset. But I'm *not* sorry I did what I did. I'm not sorry I killed him."

I glanced up in time to see Hillary spin around from the window. She still had her arms tucked tightly over her chest. To my surprise, her expression was angry.

"Sandy, you shouldn't have told us," Hillary snapped.

Sandy's eyes grew wide. He gaped at Hillary, obviously confused. "Huh? I thought—"

"You shouldn't have confessed to us," Hillary insisted. "Now you've made us all part of it. That isn't fair."

"But—but . . . you're my *friends*!" Sandy stammered, taking a few steps toward Hillary, his arms outstretched.

Hillary stepped back until she bumped against the windowsill. Her eyes were lost for a moment behind a curtain of light reflected in her glasses. She moved, and her angry glare came into view.

"It isn't right," she told Sandy through gritted teeth. "Even if we are your friends, how can you involve us in a murder? What are we supposed to do? Just keep the secret and never think about it again?"

"But I did it especially for you, Hillary!" Sandy cried hoarsely. We heard a noise outside the den door—and all of us turned. Sandy went white. I'm sure he thought his mom was at the door.

It must have been a car or something out on the street. The door remained closed.

Sandy turned back to Hillary. "Why are you giving me a hard time? I did it especially for you," he repeated shrilly. "Al was ruining your life more than anyone's. He was blackmailing you and forcing you to give him money, and—and . . ."

Hillary shook her head, frowning at Sandy.

"You should thank me!" Sandy protested. "You really should, Hillary. Instead of staring at me like that, you should be thanking me!"

"But you *killed* him, Sandy!" Hillary cried in a trembling, emotional voice I'd never heard from her before. "You *killed* him! He was ruining my life, true. He was pestering me all the time. Demanding things. Annoying me. But—"

Hillary took a deep breath. "But I would never *kill* him! Don't you get it, Sandy? Don't you see what you've done? You killed a human being. You killed *Al*!"

Sandy opened his mouth to reply. But Hillary cut him off with a sharp wave of her hand.

"You don't kill someone just because he's annoying you," Hillary said, speaking slowly, saying each word clearly and distinctly. "And then you don't confess. You don't tell what you did to a roomful of people."

"You're not *people*—" Sandy insisted. "You're my *friends*. I told you because you're my friends."

"And what are friends for?" Vincent broke in. He may have meant it as a joke, but it fell flat.

Even Vincent couldn't make us smile now. I studied him, wondering what he was really thinking. It was so hard to know with Vincent. His jokes always covered up his true feelings.

"You put us in a horrible position, Sandy." Hillary sighed, finally lowering her arms to her sides. "Now we have no choice. We have to tell your parents. Or call the police."

"No!" Taylor shrieked. She turned on Hillary. "What are you *saying*? We've got to protect Sandy. We've got to keep his secret."

"I trusted you guys," Sandy murmured, lowering his eyes to the carpet.

"I think Taylor is right," I said thoughtfully. "We can't turn Sandy in. It—it's just too horrible to think about!" For a second, I could feel myself about to burst into tears.

It was all too much. Too much sadness. Too much horror. Too much tension.

"He's made us part of a murder," Hillary argued.

"But he did it for us," Vincent chimed in. "Believe me, when Al totaled my parents' car, I wanted to kill him. I really wanted to. But I didn't have the nerve."

"You didn't want to take a human life," Hillary told Vincent. "You weren't being a wimp. You knew you don't just kill someone because they're trouble."

Taylor stepped up beside Sandy and slid her arm around his waist. "We have to go on with our lives," she said, leaning her head against Sandy's shoulder. "We have to try to forget this happened and go on with our lives. If we turn Sandy over to the police, how can we do that? How can we ever get back to normal?"

"She's right," I argued. "If we turn Sandy in, one more life will be ruined."

"Thanks, Julie," Sandy said softly. He turned to the others. "You all know me. You know I'm a good guy. You know I'm not a killer. I'm just a normal guy. And I'm your friend. We're all good friends."

He swallowed hard. I could see he was choked with feeling.

Taylor squeezed his waist. She raised her head and kissed his cheek.

"You know I'm not a killer," Sandy repeated, his eyes moving around the room. "You know I'll never ever kill again. Right? *Right?*"

A week later, Sandy killed again.

13

Sandy killed again. But this time it was in a dream I had.

In the dream, Hillary and I were running through an endless green field. And then suddenly we were skating. Gliding over the field, faster and faster, our bodies leaning into a strong breeze that fluttered our hair and our sweaters.

I remember thinking how strange it was that we could skate so well on grass. And then in the dream, the sky darkened. The grass turned blue, then black as deep shadows swept over us.

We were running again. Running in fear now. I didn't know what we were afraid of—until I saw Sandy step out from the trees.

He raised his hands. He held two Rollerblades, laced together. He pulled the skates apart and snapped the laces tight.

I'll never forget the terrifying sound of that *snap*.

I knew he was waiting to strangle Hillary and me. Strangle us both.

But we kept running toward him anyway. As if cooperating with him. As if helping him murder us.

We ran toward Sandy. He snapped the laces tight again.

And I woke up. Drenched in sweat. My nightshirt stuck against my skin.

Blinking myself alert, I heard the *snap, snap, snap* of the laces.

And slowly realized I was hearing the snap of the venetian blinds as the wind tossed them against the frame of my bedroom window.

I shivered. Picturing Sandy. Chubby little Sandy with his round, baby face.

Now he was evil. Now he was an evil figure, come to scare me in my dreams.

I squinted at the clock radio on my bed table. Only six fifteen. The sky outside the window was still gray.

I lowered my feet to the floor and started to climb out of bed. I knew I couldn't get back to sleep. I didn't *want* to go back to sleep.

I didn't want to dream again.

• • •

I told Hillary about the dream after graduation rehearsal the next evening.

Graduation rehearsal! Do you believe it?

There are nearly three hundred seniors at Shadyside High. And I don't think any of us actually believed we were graduating in a few weeks.

We all acted as if it were a big joke at rehearsal. So much joking and goofing on each other, it was more like a free-for-all!

Mr. Hernandez shouted his head off, but he couldn't get us to quiet down or line up or anything. Finally Ricky Shore stepped up to the auditorium mike and boomed at the top of his voice: "Let's get ready to rummmmmmmble!"

We all laughed. But for some reason, we also got quiet. The principal thanked Ricky for his help, ordered him off the stage, and started telling us what we had to do.

Of course, we all sang the Shadyside High alma mater off-key, howling like dogs and laughing our heads off. And then some of the guys on the football team started blocking each other when it was time to line up. And that started more laughing and shouting.

I guess we acted more like the kindergarten class than the senior class. But I think part of the reason was that most of us don't really want to graduate.

We don't want to leave Shadyside High. It's been our home for four years. We've had so many good times here. And we know that after we graduate, we won't be together like this with all our friends—ever again.

The rehearsal ended a little after eight o'clock. All over the auditorium, kids were picking up their backpacks, preparing to go home and do their homework. Even though we're almost out of here, we still have term papers to write and final exams.

Across the room near the stage, I glimpsed Vincent. He was performing for a group of girls. Some kind of wild dance, flinging his arms up in the air, shaking his whole body.

They were laughing and shaking their heads. One of them tried dancing with him but couldn't keep up. Everyone thinks Vincent is so cute—because he is.

How come he never wants to dance with *me*?

I hoisted up my backpack and caught up to Hillary in front of the stage. "Wait up! What's your hurry?" I called.

She untangled her long braid from her backpack strap. "It's so hot in here," she complained. "And I didn't think rehearsal would go this long. I've got a ton of French to do."

Hillary narrowed her eyes at me. She picked a

white ball of lint off the front of my tank top. "How come you look so tired, Julie?"

"I didn't sleep very well last night," I told her, surprised that it showed. That's when I told her about my Sandy dream and the *snap, snap* of the blinds.

She shuddered. "I can't stop thinking about it, either," she confessed. "I mean, every time I run into Sandy now, I feel kind of sick. I get this heavy feeling in my stomach."

"I know," I agreed, pressing my back against the front of the stage to let some kids squeeze past. "When I see him, I think, 'You're not Sandy anymore. You're a murderer. You're not the guy I used to know, the guy I used to like.'"

"I—I guess I feel especially bad," Hillary stammered, "because he thinks he did it for me. He thinks I *wanted* someone to kill Al." She sighed. "I thought we knew Sandy. How could someone we know so well be a . . . *killer*?"

I didn't have an answer to that question. "I agree with you now," I told Hillary. "I mean, about him confessing to us. At first, I thought it was okay. But now I'm sorry he decided to tell us."

"It's like the secret is inside me," Hillary said. "It's growing . . . growing. It's bursting to get out. It was so unfair of Sandy. So totally unfair."

"And now he comes to graduation rehearsal, and goofs with everyone, and kids around, and acts as if everything is fine," I continued. "If he can get over it, why can't we?"

Hillary started to reply—but stopped with her mouth open.

A shadow fell over us.

Someone was standing above us on the stage. I realized it at the same time as Hillary.

I turned. Raised my eyes.

And saw Taylor.

Half-hidden by the heavy, maroon curtain. She ducked quickly out of sight as I turned.

Taylor.

Hillary and I exchanged glances. I knew the same questions were in our minds:

How long had she been standing there? What had she heard?

Had she heard everything we said about Sandy?

Would she tell him?

I felt a cold shiver roll slowly down my back.

If she did tell him, what would Sandy do?

14

'm actually afraid of Sandy now," I told Hillary. "I'm afraid of what he's thinking. Of what he might do."

We were walking down Park Drive, heading toward our houses. I didn't feel like waiting for the bus. It came only once every half hour this time of night. And I suddenly felt eager to get away from the school.

"How can he sleep at night?" I asked her. "How can he say good morning to his mom and dad, knowing what he did? How can he come to school and kid around? How can he concentrate on his work? If I—if I killed someone, I wouldn't be able to do anything. My life would be over."

"I know what you mean," Hillary said, adjusting her backpack on her shoulders. "It's hard to trust him now. It's hard to think of him as a friend.

Because there's some secret part of him we didn't know about. A hard, cold part of him that's . . . that's really frightening."

We walked on in silence for a while. Our shoes thudded softly on the sidewalk. A car with only one headlight rolled past. The newly unfurled leaves on the trees trembled in a soft, warm breeze. A beautiful crescent moon tilted low over the houses up ahead.

I noticed all these things. I seemed to be super alert. As if all my senses were working overtime.

"We can't be his friends anymore," Hillary uttered, so quietly, I thought she might be talking to herself. "I mean, it can never be like it was before. For any of us."

I shook my head. "If Taylor tells Sandy what she heard us saying about him," I replied solemnly, "he won't *want* to be our friend."

We crossed the street and stepped into a wide pool of darkness. Two of the streetlights were out, I saw. The front yards stood under a heavy blanket of blackness.

I'm not sure when I became aware that we were being followed.

I think when Hillary and I stopped at the corner, I heard the scrape of a shoe on the pavement behind us.

I didn't pay any attention to it then. But when we hesitated before stepping into the darkness of the next block, I heard the scrape again. And the rustling of a hedge.

And I knew someone was behind us. Someone was watching us.

As we passed a flat, empty lot, dark weeds rustling in the heavy blackness, I grabbed Hillary's arm. Signaled for her to stop.

"There's someone back there," I whispered. "Someone following us."

"I know," she whispered back.

I heard the hedge rustle again. Heard the soft *thud* of a shoe against the ground.

I could feel Hillary's arm muscles tense. I saw her jaw clench.

We both spun around quickly.

And gasped in surprise.

15

No one there.

The wind rattled the tall hedge at the corner. Something—a tiny creature—scampered silently across the street. A chipmunk? A mouse?

Hillary and I froze in place, staring toward the corner. I held my breath. And listened.

Listened for another soft *thud*. Listened for a breath, a cough, a sigh.

And heard only the whisper of the new leaves. And the high wail of an ambulance siren somewhere far in the distance.

For some reason, Hillary and I both burst out laughing.

Loud, relieved laughter.

"Are we both going totally paranoid?" I cried.

"We're losing it," Hillary agreed. "We are definitely losing it."

"I mean, why would anyone follow us?" I added. "What on earth were we thinking of?"

I took a final squint at the hedge. It hovered over the grass, silent and still. Then I turned and led the way down the block.

"Come study at my house," I urged Hillary. "We can do all the French verbs together. It will be easier with two people."

I still felt tense. Kind of messed up and frightened. I really didn't feel like being alone.

Hillary hesitated, then said yes. "I can't stay too late, Julie. And you've got to promise one thing."

"What's that?" I asked.

"We won't talk any more about Sandy and Al."

"That's a promise," I quickly assured her.

It was a promise I couldn't keep.

As we turned the corner onto Fear Street, my house came into view. First I saw the black-and-white police cruiser in the driveway. Then I saw the policeman making his way slowly to the front door of my house.

"What does he want?" I cried, feeling a wave of heavy dread sweep over me. "Why don't they leave me alone?"

"I guess we'll soon find out," Hillary replied softly.

● ● ●

I had a strong urge to turn around, to run the other way before the policeman saw me. But Hillary and I didn't run. We made our way up the front lawn and caught up to him as he raised his hand to ring the doorbell.

I recognized Officer Reed.

"My parents aren't home!" I cried. A lie. It just burst out of me.

I wanted him to go away. I didn't want to answer any more questions.

Officer Reed turned to face us. His bald head reflected the glow from the porch light. He wore a blue police uniform, the pants wrinkled, the jacket rumpled and stained at one elbow. He was bigger than I remembered. The uniform jacket stretched tight across his stomach. His dark tie slanted crookedly. He carried his uniform hat in one hand.

I glanced at the pistol in a short brown holster at his waist. I wondered if he had ever shot anyone.

"I was hoping to see you," he said to me after nodding at Hillary. "A few more questions."

"Well, my parents aren't home," I lied. "So I don't think it would be a good idea."

Please, please go away.

"I really shouldn't talk to you if they aren't here," I continued.

He blinked. Pursed his dry lips.

And the front door swung open. My mom poked her head out. "I thought I heard voices," she said, peering into the yellow porch light. When she spotted Officer Reed, her expression turned to alarm. "Is everything okay? Julie and Hillary—?"

"I just came to ask a few more questions, Mrs. Carlson," Officer Reed said, narrowing his eyes at me. "A couple of things to ask Julie, if it's okay. I promise I'll only stay a minute."

She stepped back to allow us to enter. She had a book in her hand. A Stephen King novel.

How can she be reading horror for fun when my life *is a horror novel?* I thought.

We settled in the living room. Mom took the chair in front of the window. She kept the book in her lap but folded her hands over it.

Hillary and I sat down on opposite sides of the couch. Officer Reed pulled a pencil and small notepad from his shirt pocket. Then, with a grunt, he lowered his big body onto the ottoman in front of us.

"Have you made any progress?" Mom asked the police officer from the window. "I mean, with the case."

He had his back to her. He turned his head. "A little. I think."

The words sent a cold stab of fear to my chest.

Did he suspect Sandy? Were the police getting close
to solving Al's murder?

He turned back to me. My hands were suddenly cold and clammy. I slid them under the couch
cushion to warm them.

"Julie, I had the feeling outside that you didn't
want to talk to me," he said.

"Huh?"

I wasn't expecting him to say that.

He kept his eyes locked on me, waiting for me
to give a better answer. "Is there any reason why
you might want to avoid me?"

"No," I replied, my heart pounding. "It's just . . .
well . . . it's hard to keep being reminded of what
happened."

He nodded. His eyes didn't move from my
face. "You've been back at school for a while. Your
friends have probably been talking about the murder. You've probably heard some rumors, right?"

He waited for me to reply, but I couldn't think
of anything to say.

"Have you heard any rumors, Julie? Anything
at all that you should share with me?"

"Listen, Officer Reed, forget about rumors. I
can save you a lot of time and trouble. Al's murderer was a boy in my class named Sandy Miller. He
confessed to us all last week."

16

That's what I wanted to say.

That's what I was *dying* to say!

The words were ready to pour out of my mouth in a long stream, a cleansing stream.

I'll feel so much better if I tell him, I realized. *If I tell him, it will be over.* All the fear. All the worry. All the bad dreams.

But could I do that to Sandy?

No.

Sandy had trusted us. Sandy had trusted me—with the deepest, darkest secret of his life.

And as bad as I felt, as frightened, as upset—I couldn't betray Sandy. As much as the words wanted to explode from my lips, I couldn't say them. I had to swallow them, to hold them in.

I let my gaze slide over to Hillary on the other end of the couch. I could see by her expression that she was reading my thoughts.

Hillary wanted to tell, even more than me.

Hillary was so angry at Sandy, I knew she was bursting to tell.

Hillary was more upset than any of us that Sandy had confessed to us. Right from the beginning, she was furious that Sandy had involved us.

She slid a hand up and down her long braid. The other hand silently drummed the couch arm.

Hillary wouldn't tell, I knew.

And neither would I.

Officer Reed leaned forward on the ottoman. "You must have heard some rumors," he insisted. "Your classmates—they must have some thoughts about who murdered Al Freed."

I shook my head. "Everyone is terribly upset," I told him. "I mean, no one can believe it. It's all so unreal."

"Kids don't talk about it that much," Hillary broke in. Her voice sounded tense and tight. "It's too frightening. We all talk about graduation and stuff. I think we all want to forget, want to shove the whole thing to the back of our minds."

"She's right," I quickly agreed. Hillary was so smart. She could always put things into words better than me. "It's supposed to be a happy time. For us seniors, I mean. People don't want to be reminded that something so horrible happened. That's why I acted a little unhappy to see you at the front door."

Officer Reed nodded grimly. He rubbed his broad forehead. Then he lowered his eyes to the little notepad. "Let me run a few names by you. See if they mean anything to you."

He slowly read off a list of six or seven boys' names. None of the boys were from Shadyside High. Hillary and I had never heard of any of them.

"Are those Al's friends from Waynesbridge?" I asked.

Officer Reed tucked the notebook into his shirt pocket. "Yeah. Some of them."

"He never brought them around," I told him. "He mostly hung out with them in Waynesbridge."

"I see." The police officer pulled himself to his feet. "That's all for now," he said. "Sorry to take up your time." He nodded to my mother, who remained by the window.

"Sorry we weren't any help," I said, showing him to the front door. "If I hear anything . . ."

"Please call," he said. "Good night, everyone." He stepped out the door.

I watched from the doorway until he climbed into his cruiser. I felt so relieved. Relieved that he was leaving. Relieved that I had fought down my urge to tell him the truth, to tell him everything I knew.

His car door slammed. The headlights flashed on. A few seconds later, he pulled silently away.

When he was out of sight, I closed the front door. As I returned to the living room, my heartbeat slowed to a normal pace, my hands felt warm again.

"I hope he finds the murderer soon," Mom said, biting her bottom lip.

"I hope so," I echoed.

Mom stood up. She raised her book. "I'm going upstairs to read. I can't put this book down, even though it's scaring me to death." She said good night to Hillary and headed up to her room.

I waited till she was upstairs. Then I whispered to Hillary, "Were you thinking what I was thinking?"

"You mean about telling the policeman what we know?"

I nodded. "It was on the tip of my—"

I stopped when I saw a flash of movement through the living room window. Just the flicker of a shadow. A darting move. Out in the front yard.

I cut the lights. Then, in total darkness, stepped up to the window—and saw him. Saw him clearly.

Sandy.

"Ohhh." I uttered a low cry and motioned for Hillary to join me. We both cupped our hands around our eyes to see better.

"It's Sandy," I whispered. "Hiding behind the tree."

"Someone *was* following us!" Hillary exclaimed in a whisper. "It was Sandy."

"What is he doing out there?" I demanded. "Does he think we told Officer Reed about him? Does he think we turned him in?"

Hillary didn't reply.

We both stared out at him. Lurking behind the fat tree trunk, moonlight trickling along the ground in front of him, his face nearly hidden in blue shadows.

"He . . . he's so creepy," Hillary whispered.

"Why is he just standing there?" I wondered. "Is he *trying* to scare us? What is he doing out there? *What?*"

17

We ran to the door. We called to Sandy.

"Sandy! Sandy!" I leaned out into the darkness, shouting his name.

He didn't answer.

I saw him pull back into the deep shadows.

"Where is he?" Hillary whispered. "What is he doing?" Her voice cracked. I guess she was afraid.

Afraid of Sandy. I was too. Suddenly afraid of our old friend. Our old friend acting so strangely. *Trying* to frighten us.

"There he goes," I whispered back.

We both saw him, ducking low, staying against the hedge, running away down the block.

Hillary and I watched him until he disappeared around the hedge. I shivered as I shut the door.

Why did he do that? Why did he follow us? What did he want?

"Weird," I muttered. "Totally weird."

I didn't know that this was only the beginning. Two days later, Sandy frightened us again.

I was passing the gym after school. The double doors were open. I heard someone call my name.

I saw a bunch of guys messing around on the gym floor, passing around a basketball, dribbling and taking wild shots. "Hey, Julie—how's it going?" Vincent called.

Behind him, Sandy leaped up, tried for a slam dunk—and missed. Laughter rang out. I saw Sandy scowl. Another guy went after the ball. But Sandy cut him off and angrily grabbed it away.

"We're just goofing around," Vincent called. "Wait up and I'll walk home with you."

I felt my heart jump. Vincent wanted to walk home with me? Was he suddenly starting to catch my vibes?

He probably wants to borrow my history notes, I thought with a sigh. But I tossed down my backpack and leaned against the tile gym wall, watching them play.

The guys all seemed to be having fun. They were just dribbling and shooting, taking crazy shots, mostly missing. No one seemed to be taking it seriously—except for Sandy.

A few minutes later, Sandy and Vincent grabbed for the ball together. Vincent said something to Sandy. I couldn't hear what he said.

Sandy stopped dribbling. He gave Vincent a hard shove with both hands.

Vincent's mouth opened in shock. "Hey—I was only kidding!" he protested to Sandy.

Sandy scowled at him and returned to his dribble. Vincent took off after Sandy. He bumped Sandy from behind. Still joking around, I think.

Sandy shouted a curse as Vincent stole the ball from him.

Some of the other guys laughed. "What a klutz!" one of them shouted to Sandy.

"Butterfingers!" another boy yelled.

Sandy didn't laugh. His face turned bright red. I sucked in my breath. He suddenly looked scary.

I don't think Vincent realized how angry Sandy was. Vincent spun around and gleefully twirled the ball in Sandy's face. He held the ball out to Sandy, then pulled it away.

I gasped as Sandy let out a scream. He went into a rage. Totally lost it.

With another loud curse, he grabbed the ball

from Vincent's hand. I saw Vincent's mouth drop open in surprise. Vincent started to back away.

And Sandy heaved the ball at him with all his strength.

"Noooo!" I let out a frightened wail and ran onto the court.

Vincent let out a groan and sank to his knees. I saw him struggle to breathe. His face was bright purple.

He toppled facedown onto the floor. I bent over him, shook him, repeated his name.

The other players all gathered around. Everyone but Sandy. I glimpsed him stomping away, still red-faced, muttering under his breath. He never turned back.

Vincent groaned. He blinked his eyes.

The ball had knocked his breath out. But he was okay.

He blinked some more, gazed around. Searching for Sandy, I think. "Some friend," Vincent mumbled, shaking his head. "Some friend."

Sandy isn't *our friend anymore,* I thought bitterly, helping Vincent up.

Sandy is our enemy.

Saturday night, Hillary and I planned to go see the new Bradley Cooper film at the mall. I called

Vincent to see if he wanted to join us. "I'm meeting Hillary at the mall. We're going to an eight o'clock show. Can you come?"

Please come, I thought.

I need someone to cheer me up.

I need *you* to cheer me up.

"I can't," he said. "My parents are still being jerks. I'm still semi-grounded."

"Semi?" I asked.

"Yeah. It all depends on their mood." He groaned. "I wouldn't even bother asking them tonight. It's bad news around here. I can hear them downstairs yelling at each other right now."

"Oh." I couldn't hide the disappointment from my voice. "Well, I'd better run. I'm already late. Maybe I'll call you later?"

"Yeah. Okay. Later." He sounded really depressed.

I thought about him as I sped to the movie theater. I thought about him and Sandy and Taylor and what good times we had at the beginning of the school year. Now we were graduating, and everything seemed to be falling apart.

Normally on a Saturday night, Hillary and I would have called Sandy and Taylor. We would have made plans to meet them at the movie. Or do something else. Or go hang out with them somewhere.

But now we didn't want to see either of them.

It wasn't Taylor's fault. We didn't really have anything against her. It's just that she was always with Sandy.

And Sandy was a murderer.

Murderer. Murderer. Murderer.

As I drove, I repeated the word in my mind until it became a nonsense word. It had no meaning at all.

Murderer.

It wasn't a word I ever thought I'd use in real life. It was a word for the newspapers, for TV shows. Not for *my life*.

I shook my head hard, forcing the word from my head. The traffic on Division Street was terrible. It's usually pretty bad on Saturday night. But tonight a van had stalled in the center lane, backing up traffic for blocks and blocks.

I made it to the mall at about a minute to eight. Circled twice before I found a parking spot near the movie theater. Then I went running full speed through the lot to meet Hillary.

I found her standing beside the ticket window. She was wearing a T-shirt and an open red-leather vest over baggy black denims. "Sorry," I called breathlessly, running up to her. The lobby was nearly deserted. Everyone had gone in.

"I bought the tickets," she said, starting to

the theater door. She handed me mine. "The coming attractions started. We haven't missed anything."

"Get a seat up front," I told her. "I'll be there. I'm just going to the ladies' room."

I turned and jogged across the thick red carpet to the ladies' room against the far wall. Tucking the ticket into my jeans pocket, I pulled open the door. Stepped inside.

And bumped right into Taylor.

18

"Oh!"

We both cried out in surprise.

Then we both started talking at once:

"I didn't know you were coming!"

"I was just *thinking* about you!"

"Where are you sitting?"

"In back. On the side."

"Hillary is here too."

Taylor looked really beautiful. Her white-blond hair was pulled straight back, tied with a bright blue hair band that matched her top. She wore dark red lipstick on her full lips. Very hot and sexy.

I felt glad to see her. But the feeling lasted for only a moment. My unpleasant thoughts about Sandy washed away all my good feelings toward her.

I could see her expression change too. Her

green eyes turned cold. "Sandy and I don't see you guys very much these days," she said flatly.

I shoved my hands into my jeans pockets. "W-well, you know," I stammered. "Graduation and everything."

Lame. Really lame.

"We're graduating too," she replied sharply.

"Uh . . . we'd better get inside," I said, motioning to the door. "The movie . . . I *hate* missing the beginning. I can never catch up."

Her eyes locked on mine. She didn't move. "I thought you and Sandy were such close friends," she said.

"We were," I told her. "I mean—we *are*!" I could feel my cheeks burning. I knew I was blushing. "It's just that I've been so busy . . . and everything."

"Sandy isn't a killer!" she cried with sudden vehemence. Her eyes flashed angrily, out of control for a moment.

I gasped.

"You're supposed to be his friend," she continued, a little less heatedly. "He's kind of hurt. I mean, he thought you'd stand by him."

"I—I really have to find Hillary," I stammered. I turned to the door, desperate to get away from her.

But then I stopped. And the words burst out

of me: "Did you tell Sandy what Hillary and I were saying about him?"

Her jaw had been tightly clenched. Now her mouth dropped open. I could see red lipstick stains on her front teeth. "Excuse me?" she asked, knitting her pale eyebrows.

"You were listening to us. On the stage after graduation rehearsal. Did you tell Sandy what Hillary and I were saying?"

She shook her head, her mouth still open. "I don't know what you're talking about, Julie. I didn't hear you and Hillary. I usually don't go around *eavesdropping* on my friends!"

That made me feel a little better, a little relieved.

But then I realized that Taylor was lying.

I could see it in those cold, green eyes.

Of course she was eavesdropping on Hillary and me. Of course she heard what we were saying about Sandy.

And of course she told him.

"Uh . . . we're missing the start," I said. "Hillary and I—we'll look for you after the movie." Another lie.

One good lie deserves another.

I turned, pushed out through the door, and hurried into the darkened theater.

• • •

On Monday night, we had another rehearsal for graduation. This was a dress rehearsal, with caps and gowns and everything.

The rehearsal went late. There was a mix-up with the caps and gowns, and several kids were handed gowns way too big for them.

Then the pianist kept messing up "Pomp and Circumstance," which sent us all into giddy hysterics. For some reason, *everything* struck us funny tonight. So we had to keep starting over.

And starting over. And starting over.

Until we were all pretty tired—tired of laughing, tired of marching around in the auditorium. Hot and sweaty in the blue gowns, which felt heavier and heavier as the night dragged on.

It was nearly eleven when I dropped Hillary off at her house. And even later when I pulled the car up my driveway.

The house was dark. Mom and Dad were visiting our cousins who lived in the Old Village. They usually leave the porch light on, but tonight they must have forgotten.

The car headlights rolled up over the garage door. I slid the gear shift into park and climbed out of the car. I found the garage door clicker under the bush where we always keep it. I clicked it, and the door slowly began to rumble up.

I set the clicker down in its hiding place under the bush. Climbed back into the car. And pulled carefully into the garage—a tight squeeze. It's only a one-and-a-half-car garage, and it's filled with lawn mowers, bikes, and other junk on both sides.

Thinking about a cold drink and a shower, I cut the engine and the headlights and climbed out of the car. The sharp aroma of paint greeted me. Dad had been painting the fence at the back of the yard.

I fumbled in my bag for the house keys as I made my way around the car to the door that led from the garage into the kitchen. It was so dark. I struggled to find the keys.

I was still grabbing around in my bag when I heard a loud rumbling sound. Then a metallic squeak. Heavy grinding.

I turned with a gasp to see the garage door closing.

"Hey—!" I cried out in surprise.

A stab of fear cut through my chest. I sucked in my breath. Stared out toward the dark driveway.

"Hey—who's there?" I cried shrilly over the heavy rumble of the sliding garage door.

I froze. Panic held me in place. I couldn't decide whether to duck under the door and escape to the driveway. Or find my keys and try to get into the house.

The door was halfway to the ground when I heard the thud of footsteps. Someone ducked into the garage.

"Who is it?" I shrieked. "What do you want?"

No reply.

I fumbled again for the keys—but the bag fell from my trembling hand. It hit the concrete garage floor. I heard the clatter of things spilling out.

But I didn't lower my gaze. I kept my eyes on the dark figure moving slowly along the side of the car.

"Hey—!" Another choked cry escaped my throat.

The heavy door thudded shut.

Silence now.

I'm trapped, I realized. I squinted along the dark garage wall shelves, searching for something I could use as a weapon. Hedge clippers. A broom handle.

Anything!

"Who *are* you? What do you *want?*" My voice trembled in terror.

A rectangle of pale moonlight washed in from the long, narrow window in the garage door. The intruder stepped into the soft glow of light.

Sandy!

"Hi, Julie. It's me," he said quietly. In the silvery light, I could see a smile on his face, a strange, unpleasant smile.

"Sandy! What's the big idea?" I cried, my fear quickly giving way to anger. "You—you scared me to death!"

He didn't reply.

I saw him bend down. He picked something up from the garage floor.

I saw a metallic glint. A flash of silver.

Sandy picked up my Rollerblades. He held them in front of him as he moved toward me.

"Sandy—stop!" I shrieked. "What are you going to do?"

19

I tried to back up but bumped into the side of the car.

He raised the Rollerblades. Raised them high over my head.

"Sandy—!" I cried, throwing up my hands to shield myself.

"You shouldn't leave these on the floor," he said softly. "Someone could trip over them." He lowered them to a shelf against the wall. "Someone could get hurt," he added in a whisper.

I let out a long breath.

He grinned at me, pleased with his sick little joke.

"You're not funny," I snapped shrilly, struggling to slow my racing heart. "Why are you trying to scare me?"

He shrugged. Then he brought his face close to mine. His dark eyes locked coldly on mine.

"Why are you trying to scare *me*?" he demanded.

"I—I don't know what you mean," I stammered. I shoved his shoulders, shoved him back with both hands.

Is this really Sandy? I wondered, staring at his cold, menacing expression. Is this *really* the guy I've been friends with since third grade?

"How could I scare *you*?" I asked.

"Talking to the police scares me," he replied sharply. "It scares me a lot."

"So you admit you were spying outside my house!" I cried. "That *was* you hiding behind the tree!"

He shrugged again. "Whatever," he murmured.

"But, Sandy—" I started.

He interrupted. "I saw the police car. I wondered what was going on. So I watched. Big deal."

"Sandy, you didn't just *happen* to be in front of my house. You followed Hillary and me home. Can't you tell the truth anymore?" I cried. "Can't you tell the truth?"

He ignored my question. He narrowed his eyes at me. "Why did you call the police, Julie? Can you answer that question for me? Why did you call them?"

"I didn't!" I snapped, more shrilly than I intended. "I didn't call them. Officer Reed—he came to my house. He was waiting for me after rehearsal.

I didn't call him. He came to ask me more questions. Haven't the police been asking *you* more questions too, Sandy?"

He nodded. "They don't quit," he said softly. "They've been back to my house too."

"They think they're getting close to solving it," I told him.

His eyes flared. "No, they're *not*! That's a lie, Julie. Don't believe that lie. They tell the TV reporters they're close to solving it. So they don't look bad on TV. But the police don't have a clue." He scowled at me, leaning close. "Unless *you* told them something."

"I—I didn't!" I managed, trying to back away. "I didn't say a word, Sandy. I swear!"

He studied my face, locked his eyes on mine, as if searching for the truth in them.

"I swear!" I repeated. I stared into his scowling face. Even in the dim light, I could see sweat dripping down his forehead.

"Look at you!" I cried. "You're totally messed up. If you thought we'd turn you in, if you think we're going to give you away to the police—why did you tell us? Why did you confess to us?"

He uttered a strangled cry. "Because I trusted you. That's why," he shouted, breathing hard. "But now . . ."

"Now *what*?" I demanded.

He shook his head. He didn't answer. "We have to get over this," he murmured finally, lowering his gaze to the floor. "Really, Julie. We have to forget this happened."

"How can we?" I cried. "The police don't let us. *You* don't let us."

"I—I'm having a party," he said, raising his eyes to me. "At my house. Next Friday. Sort of a pre-graduation party. Sort of a let's-get-back-to-normal, pre-graduation party. So . . . come about eight o'clock, okay? I'm inviting Hillary and Vincent too. And a lot of other kids."

This is unreal! I thought.

He traps me in the garage. He deliberately tries to terrify me. Then he invites me to a *party*?

I swallowed. "Uh . . . I don't think I can make it, Sandy," I told him, trying to keep my voice calm and steady.

I saw him clench his jaw. Otherwise, he didn't move.

"I have to go somewhere Friday night," I lied.

He nodded. He clenched his jaw tighter. His expression turned hard, cold. "Yeah. Right," he muttered bitterly.

"Sandy. Really—" I started.

"Right, right, right." He grabbed my arm tightly, tight enough to hurt. "I was lying about the party,

Julie. I'm not having a party. It was just a test."

"A test?" I asked, squirming to free my arm.

He nodded again. "You failed it." He shoved me away roughly. "You failed the test, Julie. But I'm warning you. You have to get over this. You and Hillary and Vincent—you all have to get over this."

I stared back at him, suddenly frightened again. He wasn't warning me—he was threatening me. Threatening us all.

"We all have to go back to the way things were," he said.

"And—and what if we can't?" I stammered, my trembling voice betraying my fear.

"I'm warning you," he repeated.

He spun away from me and clicked the garage door. The motor hummed and the door squealed, then began to rumble open.

He hunched down to duck under the door. I watched him toss the clicker at the bush beside the front walk. Then he hurried away into the night.

Leaving me in the dark garage, my arms tucked around myself, hugging myself, holding myself, struggling to stop the shivers, the shudders of fear. The cold, angry glow of Sandy's eyes lingering in my mind.

20

*H*e threatened me, too," Hillary whispered. "He came to my house, and he tried to scare me."

"He *did* scare me," I admitted.

We stood at the door of the lunchroom, holding our bag lunches, our eyes searching the tables. I spotted Sandy at a table near the window. He was talking to Taylor, who sat across from him, her back to us.

Rain pelted the windows. Over the din of voices in the crowded room, I could hear the crackle of distant thunder. The fluorescent lights were on overhead. But the gloomy gray light from outside seeped over the room.

"Where do you want to sit?" Hillary asked. She waved to Deena Martinson at the table nearest us. Deena and her friend Jade Smith were arm-wrestling, for some reason. The others at their table were laughing and cheering them on.

"Sandy sees us," I reported to Hillary. "He's looking at us. He expects us to join them."

I saw Taylor turn. Both of them were watching us now.

"Forget about it. I want to enjoy my lunch," Hillary said.

She set down her bag on a table near the front aisle and pulled out a chair. Careful not to look at Sandy and Taylor, I dropped into the chair across from her.

"Maybe they'll think we didn't see them," I said.

Hillary made a disgusted face. "I don't care what they think. I don't want to sit with Sandy. He can threaten me all he wants and tell me things have to go back to normal. He's not my friend any-more."

As I pulled the tuna sandwich from my bag, I glanced at the window. A loud crack of thunder made some kids jump. Sandy and Taylor were staring at us. Sandy was talking rapidly, angrily.

I turned back quickly to Hillary. "Sandy has gone totally psycho," I said. "He tries to scare me to death. He tries to make me think he'll hurt me if I tell the police he's the killer. Then he tells me we have to be friends again like before."

My sandwich fell apart. I tried to push the tuna back into the bread.

"No way anything will ever be the same," Hillary said, shaking her head sadly. Her long, silver earrings swayed with her. "I don't think I'll *ever* feel normal again. I can't sleep at night. I can't concentrate on my work. I—I have no appetite." She shoved her container of yogurt away.

"Hey—there's Vincent!" I cried. I raised my hand high and waved to him. "Hey, Vincent! Vincent!"

I followed Vincent's gaze. He saw Sandy and Taylor too. Then he heard me calling him and hurried over to my table. "Hey, what's up?" he asked, glancing back at Sandy.

He didn't give us a chance to answer. He leaned over the table and his expression turned serious. "You know, Sandy called me last night. He sounded really messed up. And he threatened me. Do you believe it? He threatened me."

Hillary had to go to the school administrative office after classes. She had some problem about the wrong transcripts being sent to Princeton. I decided to tag along with her.

It took longer than we thought to straighten it all out. The school was nearly deserted by the time we stepped out of the office.

Hillary was grumbling about how computers

always get everything mixed up, when we turned a corner and bumped into Taylor.

"Hi. How's it going?" I asked, trying to sound casual. I started to tell her I liked the way she had her hair pulled back. But I stopped when I saw the angry expression on her face.

And I realized that we hadn't bumped into her by accident. She'd been waiting for us.

"Sandy is really hurt," Taylor said through gritted teeth. She had fine, delicate veins at her temples, and I could see them pulsing. "You've really hurt his feelings."

"I'm sorry," I said quickly. I didn't want to fight with Taylor. I had no reason to fight with her.

To my surprise, Hillary reacted angrily. "We don't care," she told Taylor. "We don't care about Sandy's feelings. We know you still care about him. But we don't. We think Sandy is—is—"

"You don't know what you're saying!" Taylor protested. Her normally pale skin had become blotched with red. The veins pulsed and throbbed at her temples. "You don't know what a good guy Sandy is! How can you hurt him like this?"

"A good guy?" Hillary shrieked. "He's a good guy? Taylor—have you totally lost it? You know what Sandy did. You can't be *that* crazy about him. You can't think he's a good guy!"

My heart started to pound as I stared at Taylor. I realized I was shocked that she decided to confront us.

I mean, I didn't even think Taylor was *that* crazy about Sandy. Sandy really wasn't her type at all. And all the while she'd been going with Sandy, she flirted with every other guy at Shadyside High!

"Sandy did what he did for all of us!" Taylor declared, spitting the words at Hillary. "And then what do his good friends do? They turn around and pretend he doesn't exist anymore! It's—it's so disgusting, I—"

She raised tight fists. Her face blazed bright red now.

"Taylor—what are you trying to prove?" I cried. "You can't *force* us to like Sandy again! You can't *force* us to forget."

"She's right. Leave us alone," Hillary added sharply.

She tried to step past Taylor.

I gasped as I saw Taylor's eyes go wild with fury. Red-faced, exploding in rage, Taylor uttered a hoarse cry and grabbed Hillary's braid.

"Hey—!" Hillary protested.

Taylor tugged hard, snapping Hillary's head around.

And then one hand swung across Hillary's neck—and in an instant, deep scratch lines darkened across Hillary's throat.

Hillary shrieked. She grabbed Taylor around the waist with both hands. And pulled Taylor to the floor.

"Stop it! Stop it!" I wailed, watching helplessly. Gaping in shock as they wrestled on the hard floor, rolling over and over, scratching and punching, gasping and sobbing as they fought.

It took me a few seconds to get myself together. Then I bent down. Grabbed Taylor by the shoulders. And struggled with all my strength to tug her off Hillary.

"Stop it! Stop it! Taylor—please!" I pleaded.

She pulled away from me. I don't even know if she heard me.

I saw bright red blood on the hall floor. Blood smearing the front of Hillary's sweater. Blood from the scratches on her throat, I realized.

"Taylor—please! Stop! Stop it!"

Finally I shoved her off Hillary. She tumbled on her side to the floor. Scrabbled to get back.

But I stepped in front of her, blocking her way.

Hillary climbed unsteadily to her feet. She pressed one hand against the scratches on her neck. She pointed with the other, pointed frantically at Taylor. "What's your *problem*? What's *wrong* with you?"

Taylor didn't reply. She stood hunched over, gasping, wheezing loudly. Her hair fell in wet tangles over her face. Her T-shirt was torn and had dark bloodstains down the side and sleeve.

"What's your problem?" Hillary shrieked at her. "Are you crazy? Are you—"

She stopped when Taylor started to vomit.

Taylor had been leaning over, gasping, struggling to catch her breath. Now she turned around, turned her head from us, her hair still spilling over her face.

A low groan escaped her throat. And then she retched. Her whole body heaving, her hands frantically pushing her hair out of the way.

"Oh wow," Hillary murmured, shaking her head. She still had one hand pressed to her throat. "Oh wow. Oh wow."

I took a step toward Taylor. "Are you okay?"

She didn't reply.

"Taylor—are you all right?" I persisted.

She had her back turned. Her shoulders heaved one more time. Then she turned back to me for an instant.

Vomit clung to the long tangles of her hair. Her eyes were red and watery. Tears rolled down her red, puffy cheeks.

"Oh wow. Oh wow," Hillary chanted.

"Taylor—can we help take you home?" I asked softly.

She shook her head. And then lurched away from us.

I started after her, but then stopped.

Taylor started to run, bumping her shoulder on the tile wall, then swaying around a corner. She vanished from view. But I could still hear her footsteps, unsteady, running footsteps, echoing away.

I turned to Hillary. "Maybe the nurse is still here," I told her. "Someone has to look at your neck."

"It's just scratches," she replied shakily. She blinked several times. Then she bent down and picked up her glasses from in front of a locker. "I'll clean it up when I get home."

Her braid had come undone. She pushed her hair behind her shoulders.

"I don't believe her," I said softly, gazing in the direction Taylor had run. "I didn't think she cared about Sandy this much. I really didn't."

"I don't care," Hillary snapped. "I don't care about Taylor at all. I only know one thing."

She tucked her top into her jeans. I saw that her hands were trembling. When she spoke, she forced her words out through gritted teeth.

"I only know one thing, Julie," she repeated.

"I've had enough. This was it. This was *it* for me."

She crossed the hall to her locker. I followed close behind.

"Hillary—what do you mean?" I asked.

"I'm not going to keep Sandy's secret any longer," she replied. "I'm not going to let him ruin my life."

I stared at her in surprise. I could see that she was serious.

"What are you going to do?" I asked.

"I'm going to tell the police," she said. "As soon as I get home."

21

I argued with Hillary as we crossed the student parking lot, ducking our heads in the rain, hurrying to my car. I'm not sure why I argued.

A lot of the time, I was tempted to call the police too. I felt as if the secret were burning a hole in my chest. Sometimes I felt that I'd never breathe normally again—unless I let the secret out, unless I told the truth to someone.

But now, as I slid behind the driver's wheel, wiping raindrops from my eyebrows, I found myself arguing with Hillary, pleading with her not to call the police.

Why? Because it was Sandy, my old friend from third grade?

Maybe.

Or was it because Sandy had involved us all? Because we were all part of Al's murder now, and telling the police the truth would set off some kind of chain reaction that would affect us all?

Maybe to that question too.

Maybe. Maybe. Maybe. As I said, I'm not really sure why I argued with Hillary. But I did.

"Al is dead," I told her. "Turning in Sandy won't bring Al back."

"I don't care," Hillary muttered, staring straight out the windshield, legs pulled up tightly, propped on the dashboard.

"Sandy's life will be ruined," I continued, turning onto Hawthorne.

The windshield wipers scraped in a steady rhythm. The rain had slowed to a drizzle.

"His life will be over."

"Good," Hillary snapped. "He killed someone, Julie. Then he practically bragged to us about it. Like he wanted extra credit or something."

"That's not why he confessed to us," I protested.

"Then why did he do it?" she demanded, her voice tense and angry.

"He wanted us to know the truth," I replied.

"Why?"

"Because . . . he trusted us and thought we should know what really happened."

"But why?" Hillary repeated impatiently. "Don't you see, Julie—he could have kept it to himself. It wouldn't have made it any different to us. Al was dead. Somebody killed him. No one knows who. So why was Sandy so eager to confess to us?"

I opened my mouth to reply. But I didn't really have an answer.

"Because he wanted us to admire him," Hillary answered her own question. "He wanted us to congratulate him. He wanted us to say he was a hero. And especially, he wanted Taylor to think he was a big macho hero."

I gasped. "You don't think he killed Al just to impress Taylor!"

Hillary shook her head. Behind her glasses, her eyes remained half shut, thoughtful.

"No. I think he killed Al because Al humiliated and embarrassed him in front of Taylor. And because Al was bullying us all and making all our lives miserable."

She took a breath. "But," she continued, "I think Sandy *confessed* to us because he was trying to impress Taylor."

"And it worked," I said, sighing. "Now Taylor is so nuts about him, she's ready to fight anyone who hurts Sandy's feelings. I can't believe she started that fight with you over *nothing*!"

Hillary didn't reply. I could see she was thinking hard. And by the determined expression on her face, I could tell that my arguments weren't going over.

"I'll say it one more time," I told her, switching off the wipers. I turned on the headlights. Even though it was only four thirty, the overcast sky was already as dark as night.

"Sandy did a horrible thing," I continued. "And it's horrible that we know about it. But turning him in to the police will only ruin his life. It won't do any good. You and I—we're really upset. But we know that Sandy isn't really a murderer. We know he's never going to murder again. So is it right to ruin his life just because you're upset about knowing his secret? And upset about Taylor?"

Hillary let her feet slide to the floor. She turned to me. "I'm not so sure," she said.

I slowed to a stop at a red light. The rain started up again. "Not so sure what?"

"Not so sure he won't kill again," she replied.

"Hillary, really—" I started.

"He's threatening us," Hillary continued. "He's trying to scare us. He's trying to bully us into pretending nothing ever happened. He's out of control, Julie." She swallowed hard, then pressed her palm against her injured throat. "What makes you think he won't kill again?"

I didn't know how to answer. Maybe she was

right. I squinted into the rain. The wipers smeared the glass, making it hard to see.

"Turn around," Hillary ordered urgently. "Turn the car around!"

"Huh?" She startled me. "What's wrong?"

"I changed my mind," she said, sitting up straight. She brushed back her hair. "I don't want to go home. Take me to Sandy's house."

"Whoa!" I cried. "Hillary, what on earth . . . ?"

"You convinced me," she said. "I won't go straight to the police. I want to talk to Sandy first. Reason with him. Maybe I can convince Sandy to go to the police. You're right, Julie. Sandy *is* our old friend, after all. I owe it to him. I have to give him a chance to do the right thing."

I turned into a driveway, then backed out, turning the car toward Sandy's house on Canyon Road. "I'll go with you," I said.

"No." Hillary squeezed my shoulder. "Thanks. But no. I want to talk to Sandy by myself. If we both go, it might set him off. He might think we're ganging up on him."

"But, Hillary—"

"No," she insisted firmly. "I mean it. I'm going in to talk to him by myself."

"Then I'll wait outside for you in the car," I offered.

She shook her head again. "Go home, Julie. I'll call you as soon as I get home. I promise."

A few minutes later, I pulled the car up Sandy's driveway and watched Hillary dart through the swirling rain to the front door. The door opened after a few seconds. Hillary disappeared inside the house.

I waited for a minute or two. Listening to the scrape of the windshield wipers over the hum of the car engine. Staring through the spotted glass at the closed front door.

For a moment, I felt tempted to disobey Hillary's instructions. To climb out of the car. To follow her into Sandy's house. To stand beside her as she confronted him.

But I fought back the urge. Dropped the gearshift into reverse. Backed down the drive and obediently headed for home.

Several times I felt tempted to turn around and go back to Sandy's.

Why do I have this heavy feeling of dread? I wondered, moving the car through the gray evening, through the pelting sheets of rain.

Why do I feel so upset, so worried?

Why do I feel that something *horrible* is about to happen?

Three hours later I had the answer.

22

planned to hurry home and wait for Hillary's call. But the rain had the cars backed up on Mill Road. And it seemed to take forever to get to Fear Street.

As I turned onto my block, the old trees that hang over the street cut off the remaining light. Dark as midnight now.

Why do I have to live on Fear Street? I asked myself.

My friends all teased me about it. Everyone tells horrifying stories about Fear Street and the frightening things that supposedly happened there.

I don't think it's scary. It's just *darker* than everywhere else because of all the old trees.

I finally pulled up the driveway, my tires crunching heavily over the wet gravel—and saw

Mom's car in the garage. *She's home early,* I realized. I hoped nothing was wrong.

I found her in the kitchen. "Mom?" Even with her back turned to me, I could see instantly that she was crying.

"Mom? Mom? What's wrong?"

"I'm chopping onions," she replied, turning to me with a smile. "Everyone says to hold your breath or close your eyes. But nothing works. I cannot chop onions without crying."

I let out a sigh of relief. I was sure Mom had had some horrible news.

I thought about Hillary at Sandy's. "Did Hillary call?" I asked my mother.

She wiped tears off her cheeks with the back of one hand. "No. You just got out of school. Why would Hillary call?"

"No reason," I replied. Rain pattered on the kitchen window. It sounded like someone knocking. I gasped and turned to the window.

"Wow. You're jumpy today," Mom commented.

"It's . . . uh . . . just the rain," I said. "How come you're home early?"

She started to chop another onion. "I had a dentist appointment at three thirty. So I decided there wasn't really time to go back to the office."

"What are you making for dinner?" I asked,

taking a Mountain Dew from the refrigerator.

"Meat loaf. Your father should be home in an hour. I thought I'd surprise him by actually cooking dinner for once."

The onions started to burn my eyes. "Can I help?" I asked, thinking about Hillary again.

"No. Not really. You can set the table later, if you want."

"Okay," I told her, blinking away onion tears. "I'm going up to my room. Maybe I'll try to do my French before dinner."

I hurried up to my room. But I didn't do my French homework.

I sat on my bed and stared at the phone beside me on the nightstand. "Come on—ring," I ordered it.

The phone didn't obey.

Where is Hillary? I wondered, feeling all my muscles knot with tension. *What is taking her so long?*

I glanced at the clock radio every two minutes. Five thirty. Five thirty-two. Five thirty-four.

She should be home by now, I told myself.

I stood up. My legs felt rubbery. Weak. I started to pace back and forth, turning sharply. Not much room to pace in my little room.

Where is she? Where is she?

I started to feel guilty. I dropped Hillary off and then drove away.

What kind of friend am I?

I should have gone in with her. I shouldn't have listened to her. I should have insisted. The two of us should have confronted Sandy.

Not Hillary alone.

My stomach started to churn. My hands felt as cold as ice.

I dropped back down onto the bed. And stared at the phone.

Come on—RING!

The phone rang.

"Ohh!" I uttered a startled cry. I nearly jumped to the ceiling!

I grabbed the phone before the first ring ended. "Hello?" I called breathlessly.

"Julie?"

"Yes?"

"Hi. This is Hillary's mom. How are you?"

"Uh . . . fine, Mrs. Walker. Is Hillary—"

"Do you know where Hillary is?" Mrs. Walker asked. "I told her this morning we were having dinner at six sharp tonight because her father and I have a meeting at seven. Is she at your house?"

I swallowed hard. My mouth suddenly felt as dry as sand. "No. No, she isn't here," I replied softly.

A chill tightened the back of my neck. *Where is she? Where IS she?*

"Did she stay late at school?" Mrs. Walker asked. "I know she had a problem about some transcripts."

"I . . . I don't know," I lied. "I don't know where she is, Mrs. Walker. If I see her . . ."

"She's probably caught in traffic. Because of the rain," Hillary's mother said. "Did you ever see such a downpour?"

"It's pretty bad," I murmured, thinking about Hillary. Hillary and Sandy.

"Well, see you soon, Julie. Bye." Mrs. Walker hung up.

I shut my eyes. "Please be okay, Hillary," I whispered.

I dropped her off at Sandy's.

I dropped her off at a *murderer's* house.

And then I left her there to confront him. To tell him he had to turn himself in to the police.

What have I done? I asked myself, feeling the panic rise up from my stomach. Feeling the cold terror sweep over my body, freezing me in place.

I left Hillary alone with a murderer.

Have I sent her to her death?

Has Sandy murdered her, too?

"Dinner!" Mom's voice from downstairs broke into my frightening thoughts. "Dinner, Julie! Can't you hear me? How many times do I have to call?"

"Sorry, Mom. I'm coming now," I shouted down.

I shook my head hard as if trying to toss out the terrifying thoughts. "Julie, you're getting crazy," I scolded myself, climbing to my feet.

I was letting my imagination run away with me. Letting my wildest fears take over my mind.

No way Sandy would hurt Hillary, I assured myself.

No way. No way.

He isn't a killer. He killed Al. But that was different.

I took a deep breath and stepped over to the mirror above my dresser. I stared back at myself, pale, my eyes troubled, my dark hair disheveled.

"Julie—where are you? Dinner is getting cold!" Dad's impatient call came from downstairs.

"Com—ing!" I ran a brush quickly through my hair. Then I hurried down the stairs to dinner.

I tried to eat Mom's meat loaf and mashed potatoes. It was one of my favorite dinners. But tonight I had to choke it down.

I talked about graduation and school stuff, and tried to sound calm and normal.

But I couldn't stop thinking about Hillary. Hillary at Sandy's house. Hillary telling Sandy she planned to turn him in unless he turned himself in.

She didn't call until dinner was over and the table had been cleared.

I glanced at the clock as I ran to answer the phone. Seven fifteen.

When I picked it up, Hillary's voice sounded tiny and troubled in my ear. "Julie—?"

"Yes. Hi. What happened, Hillary? What's the story?" I demanded breathlessly.

"Julie—?" she repeated. She sounded so strange. So . . . frightened.

"Yes? What, Hillary? What?"

"Can you come over? Right now?" she asked, her voice tight, trembling.

"Huh? Come over?" I gasped. "Why? What's wrong, Hillary? What happened?"

"Something terrible," Hillary replied, lowering her voice to a whisper. "Something terrible, Julie."

Silence. I waited for her to continue.

"What's wrong?" I choked out. "What?"

"I killed him," Hillary whispered. So soft, I wasn't sure I heard correctly. "I killed him," she repeated. "I killed Sandy."

Part 3

23

How did I ever drive to Hillary's house? I don't remember being in the car. I don't remember if the rain had stopped or not. I don't remember anything about the drive.

Except my fear. And the sick feeling I kept swallowing down. And my cold, damp hands sliding over the steering wheel.

What excuse did I give my parents for rushing out on a school night?

What did I think about as I obediently hurried to Hillary's house? What did I *tell* myself?

I don't remember *anything*. My mind is a blank.

I think I wanted it to be a blank. I think I wanted to forget everything, to start my life all over again.

I didn't want to know that Al was dead. That Sandy had murdered him, strangled him in the alley with a pair of skates.

And I didn't want to know that another one of my friends had been murdered tonight. That Sandy was dead now, killed by my best friend.

Hillary, I didn't want to know.

I didn't want to remember.

But you can't keep your mind a blank forever. And as I stepped into Hillary's house, wiping my wet shoes on the welcome mat, it all burst back on me—like a high ocean wave that sweeps over you and leaves you dizzy and gasping for air.

And I uttered a choked cry. And threw my arms around Hillary's shoulders. And pressed my cold cheek against her face, startled by how burning hot her skin felt.

"I—I haven't told them yet," Hillary whispered.

"Huh?" I let go. Backed up, feeling shaky, feeling as if I could start to cry—and cry forever. Forcing down the sobs that made my chest heave.

And I saw Taylor and Vincent, standing awkwardly in the center of the living room.

A white flash of lightning at the big front window made their shadows jump. But they didn't move. Taylor wore a loose, red tank top over black pants. Her white-blond hair fell over her shoulders. She had her arms crossed over her chest.

Beside her, Vincent brushed back his rust-colored hair. I saw that it was wet, as if he'd been out in the rain a long time. He appeared even more uncomfortable than usual. He pulled his big hands from his jeans pockets, then didn't seem to know what to do with them.

He flashed me a strange look—half smile, half question. As if to say, *What's going on here? Do you know why we're here tonight?*

Of course I knew.

It was Hillary's turn to make a frightening, painful confession. Hillary's turn to throw us all into panic, into sorrow.

"How's it going?" Vincent murmured to me, clenching and unclenching his fists.

"I—I'm not sure," I stammered, glancing at Hillary.

She appeared surprisingly calm. But I could see that she'd been crying. When she caught me staring at her, she lowered her gaze to the floor, as if turning me away, shutting me out.

"Sit down, guys," she said softly. She motioned with both hands, toward the couch and chairs across from the fireplace.

A roar of thunder made me jump. I accidentally bit my lower lip. I could taste the bitter tang of blood on my tongue.

More lightning flickered, making our shadows dance. Vincent and Taylor dropped onto the couch. I sat on the edge of an armchair.

Hillary stood facing us. Lightning flashed in her glasses. She tugged nervously at her braid, rolling her hand over it, twisting it between her fingers.

"I . . . killed . . . Sandy."

She spoke the words flatly, slowly, without any emotion at all. Kept her eyes on the window.

Lightning flashed again in her glasses. As if shielding her, hiding her gaze from us.

Taylor gasped and shot up from the couch. She stumbled forward, hands raised as if to attack Hillary.

I jumped to my feet too. I'm not sure why. Did I plan to protect Hillary from Taylor?

I saw Vincent's eyes bulge as he stood behind Taylor. He didn't say a word. I don't think he believed it.

I'm not sure I believed it either.

So Hillary repeated it. "I killed Sandy. I didn't mean to. But I killed him."

"Noooooo!" A shrill animal wail escaped Taylor's lips. She dove forward and grabbed Hillary roughly by the shoulders. "Nooooo!"

I tensed and moved toward them. Was Taylor about to lose it again? Would she start another fight?

"Let me explain!" Hillary cried, raising her voice for the first time.

Startled, Taylor let go of her and stepped back.

"Sit down!" Hillary instructed sharply. "Let me explain. At least, give me a chance to explain what happened. It—it was so *horrible!*"

I dropped back onto the edge of my chair. Taylor, trembling now, glaring at Hillary, backed away. She stood in front of the couch, refusing to sit down.

Vincent uttered a sigh. Then he propped his head in his hands, leaning forward tensely, his eyes locked on Hillary.

Hillary rubbed the red, angry-looking scratches on her throat. Then she clasped her hands behind her and paced back and forth as she told us what had happened.

"I went over to Sandy's after school," she began, her eyes on Taylor. "I mean, Julie dropped me off. I—I—"

Her voice cracked.

She took a deep breath and began again. "I decided I couldn't take it anymore. Knowing what Sandy did—knowing that Sandy murdered Al—it was ruining my life. I couldn't stop thinking about it. I couldn't think about anything else. It was driving me crazy.

"Every time I saw Sandy, I felt like screaming," Hillary continued. "Every time I saw him, I felt like crying. Like grabbing him and shaking him. It—it was too much to take. Too much."

She took another deep breath. She tugged at her braid and continued to pace.

"So I went over to Sandy's this afternoon to *beg* him to go to the police. To tell them the truth. If Sandy told them that Al was blackmailing us, that he was bullying us and threatening us, that Al was ruining our lives, maybe they would understand."

Hillary uttered a loud sob. It took her a few seconds to get herself back in control. "So I begged Sandy to go to the police. But he wouldn't listen to me. He refused. Then I said if he didn't go to the police, I would. When I said that, Sandy turned violent. He—he totally lost it."

Hillary pulled a wadded-up tissue from her jeans pocket. She lifted her glasses and dabbed at her eyes with it.

"He—he went into a rage," she continued, squeezing the tissue in her hand. "I—I couldn't believe it. I never expected . . ." Her voice trailed off. She dabbed her eyes again. The tissue was crumbling in her hand.

"He picked up that heavy sculpture his mom did. You know the one of Sandy? He was screaming at me. Telling me I was going to ruin everything. He said he couldn't let me destroy his life. He—he picked up the bronze head. He raised it up high. I think he wanted to hit me with it, to bring it down on my head."

Another sob made Hillary's chest heave. But she continued to choke out her story. "I grabbed the bronze head too. It was so much heavier than I thought. Sandy and I—we wrestled around.

"I was so scared. He really wanted to hurt me. He was so out of control. So panicked. I think Sandy really wanted to *kill* me!"

I gasped. I wiped my cheeks. My face felt wet from tears. I didn't even realize I'd been crying.

Hillary dabbed her eyes one more time. Then she tossed the tattered tissue to the floor.

"Sandy was screaming at the top of his lungs," she continued. "He kept screaming, 'You can't ruin everything! I won't let you ruin everything!' Then—then . . .

"Then I grabbed the heavy sculpture away from him. And it fell. It fell onto his head. I'm not sure how. It—it caught the back of his neck. Sandy let out a cry. Just a squeak, really. A horrible squeak. I'll never forget it.

"He crumpled to the floor. The sculpture fell with him. It landed on his head. It made such a terrible cracking sound. I—I guess I was in shock or something. I'm not sure what happened next.

I guess I bent down. I pulled the bronze head off him. But . . .

"But he wasn't moving. The sculpture—it had cut open something in his neck. A blood vessel or something. Blood was spurting up from his neck—from his head. Spurting up like a water fountain.

"I tried to stop it. Really, I did. But I was so panicked. I couldn't find anything to wrap his neck with. I—I couldn't find anything to stop the bleeding.

"His skull—it was crushed. I knew it was crushed. And he just kept bleeding and bleeding. So much blood, I thought I could swim in it.

"Sandy was dead. I—I killed him. And then . . . I ran. I just ran. Ran out into the rain. Ran and ran until I got home. And then I called you."

"Noooo," Taylor moaned, hugging herself, hugging herself tightly, her eyes shut. "Noooooo."

"I killed Sandy," Hillary repeated, her voice sounding dull now, hollow. Her eyes faded, lifeless behind her glasses. "It was an accident. But I killed him."

She turned to me. "I'm going to call the police now. I'm going to call them and tell them how it happened. But I thought . . . I thought you should know first. You're my friends, and I wanted you to know the truth."

I turned as Taylor uttered a shrill shriek. "But *why*?" she said. "Why? Why? Why?"

Once again, she staggered toward Hillary. "Why did Sandy have to die? Why? Why Sandy?" she wailed.

"Taylor, I tried to explain—" Hillary started.

But Taylor's cries drowned Hillary out. "You don't understand!" Taylor screamed. "You don't understand anything at all! Why did Sandy have to die? He didn't do anything! He didn't do anything at all! Don't you understand? Sandy didn't kill Al! *I* did!"

24

I suddenly felt so dizzy, I had to slump back in the chair.

I was still shaking from Hillary's story. Still gripped with the horror of what had happened at Sandy's house. Still picturing their desperate fight, picturing Sandy on the floor, the spurting blood, the heavy sculpture cracking his skull.

Still picturing Hillary's terror—when Taylor changed it all. Changed everything. Everything. With just two sentences:

"Sandy didn't kill Al! *I* did!"

"Is it *true*?" The words burst from my throat in a dry, tight voice I didn't recognize. "*You* killed Al?"

Taylor nodded. She glared at Hillary, her green eyes flashing with fury. "You killed the wrong person, Hillary."

"It was an accident!" Hillary protested. "A horrible accident!"

I climbed to my feet. I slid an arm around Hillary's waist and led her to the couch. Vincent grabbed her hand. He squeezed it soothingly.

Hillary's whole body was shaking, as if she had a high temperature. A small, square plaid quilt was thrown over the back of the couch. I pulled it off and wrapped it around Hillary's shoulders.

"Doesn't anyone want to know *why* I killed Al?" Taylor demanded. I turned and saw that she had taken my chair. She leaned forward, hands gripping the chair arms. Leaned forward as if confronting the three of us on the couch.

"I was going out with Al," Taylor confessed. "Yeah. Yeah, I know. Behind Sandy's back. Well . . . it's too late for me to feel bad about it — isn't it?"

She uttered a bitter sigh. "I've always had a weakness for dangerous guys. And Al was kind of dangerous. A lot more exciting than Sandy, anyway. I liked Al because he was bad, he was dangerous. But Al was also trouble."

She sneered, shaking her head, eyes lowered. "A few months ago, I stole some money from my parents. About a hundred bucks. To get Al out of a jam. What a mistake. I don't know what I could have been thinking of."

She stopped talking. Her eyes watered over. Her chin trembled.

We waited for her to finish her story. We waited a long time. She appeared lost in her own thoughts.

Finally she started again. "Al was such a creep. He demanded more money. And then more money. He threatened to tell my parents that I'd stolen money from them. Even though I stole it for *him*!"

"Unreal," Vincent muttered.

He and I had our arms around Hillary, trying to calm her down.

"Such a creep," Taylor muttered. "I told him I never wanted to see him again. I never wanted him to *talk* to me again. But he forced me to meet him after we went skating that night. He pulled me into the alley. He said he needed another hundred dollars.

"I told him no way! I said, 'Go ahead and tell my parents. I really don't care anymore.'

"So then he started to get rough. He grabbed me. He slammed me against the wall at the back of the rink. I—I was really scared. He started to pull the skates from around my neck."

Taylor swallowed hard. Tears rolled down her pale cheeks. She made no effort to wipe them away.

"That's when I lost it," she continued, gripping the chair arms so tightly that her knuckles whitened. "I grabbed the skates back. We wrestled. The laces were tied together. Somehow . . . somehow they ended up around his neck. I guess I put them there. I really don't remember.

"But I remember pulling them, pulling them tight. Pulling them with all my strength. With the strength of my fury. My insane fury. Strength I didn't know I had.

"I strangled Al. I hated him so much. I went into a fury, I guess. Like a trance. As if I was blind. As if I wasn't inside me. I was on the outside, watching my body—watching *someone's* body—choke Al. Choke him. Choke him. Until he stopped struggling and didn't move anymore.

"And then . . ." She sucked in a deep breath. The tears stained the shoulders of her tank top. "And then I ran to Sandy. I told him everything."

Taylor let out a sob that made her whole body shudder. "Sandy was so wonderful. No guy ever cared about me that much. Sandy cared about me *too* much! He confessed to the murder. To save me.

"He told you that he killed Al. He knew you were his friends. He knew you wouldn't betray him. He trusted you. And—and—" Taylor's voice caught in her throat.

"And what did you do?" she managed to scream at us. "He trusted you—and you turned on him!" She glared across the room, her eyes locked furiously on Hillary. "You turned on him. And you *killed* him! How *could* you? He was innocent! He was totally innocent! How *could* you kill him?"

Taylor jumped up. She balled her hands into tight fists and started toward Hillary.

She stopped as the doorbell rang.

The sound made us all cry out.

Hillary leaped to her feet and tossed away the plaid quilt.

The doorbell rang again.

Vincent and I followed Hillary to the front door.

"Did you call the police?" Taylor demanded. "Is that who it is, Hillary? Did you call the police before you invited us over?"

Hillary didn't answer.

We stepped into the front hall.

She pulled open the door.

And Sandy walked into the house.

25

I can't tell you what happened next.

I felt so much emotion, I was dazed. The room started to spin. Lightning flashed in the open doorway, and I felt as if its white-hot current was exploding through my body. Blinding me with its brightness. Making the whole room vibrate and whirl.

And then a shrill voice broke into my consciousness.

"You *tricked* me!" Taylor shrieked.

I turned in time to see her collapse to her knees. "You *tricked* me! You *tricked* me!"

Sandy grabbed her up. He wrapped his arms around her. "I'm so sorry," he whispered. "Taylor, believe me. I'm so sorry."

He was still holding her as Hillary and I hurried to the phone to call Taylor's parents.

"Sorry I had to pretend with you, too, Julie,"

Hillary apologized, holding the phone to her ear. "I figured out the truth and confronted Sandy with it. Sandy couldn't live with the secret any longer. He and I agreed we had to shock Taylor into confessing. But I needed you to be shocked too."

"It's okay," I told her. "At least we finally know the truth."

Hillary talked to Taylor's father. She told him to hurry over.

"I owe everyone an apology," Sandy said. "I—I wanted to protect Taylor. But I don't know why I started treating you guys so badly. Following you around. Trying to scare you and everything. I guess I didn't want you to find out the truth. And I guess I wanted to show Taylor that I could be as dangerous as Al."

Sandy sighed, holding on to Taylor tightly. "I know the whole thing was crazy and stupid," he said sadly. "I never should have confessed to the murder. Never."

"I think we've had enough confessions around here to last a lifetime!" I exclaimed.

Everyone in the room agreed.

But there was one confession still to come.

Two weeks later, Vincent and I were walking home from school when he suddenly leaned close and said in a low voice, "Julie, I have a confession to make."

A confession?

Oh no! Please—no! I thought. *One more confession and I'll scream!*

I held my breath. I shut my eyes. "Confession? What's your confession?" I asked hesitantly.

"I've had a crush on you since third grade," Vincent admitted.

I screamed.

Read on for a peek
at Fear Street:

NIGHT GAMES.

Whoooa!" I stopped and grabbed Lenny Boyle's arm. "Check it *out*!"

I had to shield my eyes against the harsh, bright lights. Lenny laughed and pretended to stagger off the sidewalk.

Cassie Wylant and Jordan Townes were half a block back, arguing again. They had been fighting all night, even while they were dancing. Sometimes I wonder why Cassie and Jordan are dating. They're always breaking up, then making up, then breaking up again.

"Hellllooo!" I called, trying to get their attention. "Take a break, guys. You've got to see this!"

They stopped and gawked at the amazing sight. Even Cassie had to laugh. It's hard to get Cassie to laugh. She's a great friend, but she really doesn't have much of a sense of humor.

In fact, she's the most serious person in our crowd. Always study, study, study. It was great seeing her lighten up and dance at Red Heat tonight. Her copper-colored hair was flying. Her hazel eyes reflected the flashing lights.

If only she and Jordan didn't fight all the time.

He's so good-looking—and he knows it. And he's always coming on to other girls. I think that's what starts most of their fights. I don't know for sure.

Cassie and I are good friends. But Cassie sort of keeps herself tightly wrapped up. She doesn't reveal what she's really thinking—not even to me.

But now, walking home from the dance club, we were all thinking the same thing: How could Mr. Crowell do this to his front yard?

All four of us stopped and stared at the brightest, ugliest, craziest, *tackiest* display of Christmas lights we'd ever seen! Red and green lights blazed from the roof, around the windows and doors, along the gutters—and in all the trees!

Mr. Crowell had *two* Santas facing each other in identical, glowing sleighs. Reindeer with flashing red noses, elves, gremlins, Santa's helpers, bright purple mice, bright white snowmen, neon animals I didn't even recognize—and twinkling, flashing, glowing lights *everywhere*!

"It's brighter than the dance club!" Jordan

declared, shaking his head. His dark eyes twinkled too, reflecting the red glare of the lights.

"He'll need a calculator to add up his electric bill!" I chimed in.

Everyone laughed. You see, Mr. Crowell is our math teacher. And he doesn't allow us to bring calculators to class.

Lenny scowled. "We should smash them," he muttered.

Mr. Crowell is *not* Lenny's favorite teacher.

In fact, Mr. Crowell isn't *anyone's* favorite teacher.

Every school has at least one teacher that everyone hates. At Shadyside High, Mr. Crowell wins that prize.

I'm so easygoing and sensible, I get along well with all my teachers. All except Mr. Crowell.

Diane Browne, please complete this equation to the fifth decimal. I can hear his high, shrill voice. It always gives me chills, like chalk scraping on a blackboard.

I snuggled against Lenny. We were both glowing from the lights of the front yard. The tiny stud in Lenny's ear sparkled like a star. I kissed his cheek.

Poor Lenny. Mr. Crowell was toughest on him.

All the teachers were tough on Lenny. I guess

because Lenny doesn't care much about school. Because he doesn't play the game. Because he's kind of tough-looking.

Why do I go out with a guy like Lenny? A quiet, sensible girl like me?

Because I know him well enough to get past his surface cool. Because I know he's a really good guy underneath. He acts tough—but he's really a marshmallow.

Actually, I'm surprised that Lenny wants to go out with *me*. I'm not as pretty as a lot of girls. I mean, I'm not as pretty as Cassie, for example. My blond hair is kind of scraggly and my nose is a little crooked. And I can't afford really nice clothes.

But Lenny and I have a good time together. When he's not in one of his angry moods. Those times when he gets low, there isn't much I can do. Just wait for him to come out of it.

"I can't believe that a total *grump* like Crowell has so much Christmas spirit!" Cassie exclaimed.

"Did you ever see anything so ugly?" Jordan demanded, grinning. "I *love* it! I want to do this in *my* front yard. I'd keep it going all year!"

I laughed. Cassie shook her head disapprovingly. "You have no taste," she said softly.

"I know," Jordan shot back. "That's why I go out with *you*!"